"You should come to London," she said. "You'd be snapped up."

"Not much point if the woman doing the snapping doesn't fancy the idea of life on a farm," said Bram. "A girl who hates cold mornings and mud is no good to me. That's obviously where I've been going wrong all these years. All my girlfriends have been town girls. What I need is a country girl."

Sophie looked at him affectionately. Yes, a nice country girl was exactly what Bram needed. Surely there was someone out there who would be glad to make a life with Bram? On winter nights she could draw the thick, faded red curtains in the sitting room against the wind and rain and sit with Bram in front of the fire, listening to it spit and crackle.

"I wish I could marry you," she said with a wistful smile.

Bram put down his mug. His mother's clock ticked into the sudden silence.

"Why don't you?" he said.

Jessica Hart was born in West Africa, and has suffered from itchy feet ever since, traveling and working around the world in a wide variety of interesting but very lowly jobs, all of which have provided inspiration to draw on when it comes to the settings and plots of her stories. Now she lives a rather more settled existence in York, England, where she has been able to pursue her interest in history, although she still yearns sometimes for wider horizons. If you'd like to know more about Jessica, visit her Web site www.jessicahart.co.uk

Books by Jessica Hart

HARLEQUIN ROMANCE®
3844—HERE COMES THE BRIDE (2-in-1 with Rebecca Winters)
3861—CONTRACTED: CORPORATE WIFE

Don't miss any of our special offers. Write to us at the following address for information on our newest releases.

Harlequin Reader Service
U.S.: 3010 Walden Ave., P.O. Box 1325, Buffalo, NY 14269
Canadian: P.O. Box 609, Fort Erie, Ont. L2A 5X3

MISTLETOE MARRIAGE

Jessica Hart

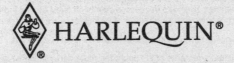

TORONTO • NEW YORK • LONDON
AMSTERDAM • PARIS • SYDNEY • HAMBURG
STOCKHOLM • ATHENS • TOKYO • MILAN • MADRID
PRAGUE • WARSAW • BUDAPEST • AUCKLAND

ISBN 0-373-03869-0

MISTLETOE MARRIAGE

First North American Publication 2005.

www.eHarlequin.com

Printed in U.S.A.

CHAPTER ONE

BRAM was unloading bales when Sophie found him.

It was a delicate business to lift each bale from the back of a trailer, and she watched him for a while as he stacked them carefully outside the farm shed, marvelling affectionately at how calm and methodical he was about everything.

There was something almost graceful about the way the tractor moved backwards and forwards in a slow and cumbersome ballet, and Sophie began to feel calmer. She waved to attract Bram's attention the next time he turned his head, and he stopped at the sight of her, hunched in her jacket, the cold wind blowing her unruly curls around her face.

'Hello!' He jumped down from the tractor, followed by the ever-faithful Bess, who ran over to greet Sophie, wriggling and squirming with pleasure in a manner quite unbefitting a sheepdog as she bent to pat her. 'I didn't know you were coming up.'

'It was a spur-of-the-moment thing,' said Sophie, straightening.

She had decided to come home the moment her mother had told her that Melissa and Nick were on holiday. Although now she wished she hadn't.

'I'm just here for the weekend.'

'Well, it's good to see you.' Bram enveloped her in a hug. 'It's been too long.'

Bram's hugs were always incredibly comforting. By rights they ought to be bottled and handed out to the lonely and the heartbroken, Sophie always thought. When he held you enclosed in those powerful arms you felt safe and secure, and insensibly steadied. He didn't need to say a thing. You could just cling to his strong, solid body and feel the slow, calm beat of his heart and somehow let yourself believe that everything would be all right.

'It's good to see you too,' she said, hugging him back and smiling up at her oldest friend with unshadowed affection.

By unspoken agreement they moved over to the gate that looked out over the wide sweep of moor. It was just the right height for leaning on, and in the past they had had many discussions with their arms resting on it.

'So, how are things?' asked Bram.

Sophie's reply was a grimace.

'What's the matter?'

'Oh…everything,' she sighed.

Careless of the green mould, Sophie folded her arms on the top bar of the gate and gazed across the valley at the moor opposite. It looked bleak and brown on this raw November afternoon, but at least you could breathe up here. She thought of the small flat she shared in London, where the only view was of concrete backyards or the busy road where traffic growled through the night.

She took a deep breath. She could smell heather and sheep and the faint autumnal tang of woodsmoke drifting up from the village nestled into a fold at the foot of the moors, and she felt the tension inside her ease as her shoulders relaxed slightly, almost in spite of herself.

It was always the same at Haw Gill Farm. There was something about the air up here, high in the moors. She would arrive in state of turmoil, feeling desperate and churning with drama and emotion, but a few breaths and somehow things wouldn't seem so bad.

'Just the usual, then?' said Bram, and the corner of Sophie's mouth lifted at his deadpan tone.

Typical Bram. Nothing ever shocked him or startled him or enraged him. It was amazing that they had been friends for so long when they were so different. She was chaotic and turbulent; he had raised understatement to an art form. He was thoughtful and considered, while she was prone to excitement and exaggeration. Sometimes he drove her crazy with his placidity, but Sophie knew no one more steadfast or more true. Bram was her rock, her oldest friend, and he always made her feel better.

'Don't make me laugh,' she complained. 'I'm not supposed to be feeling better yet. Not until I've had a good moan and told you what the matter is!'

'*Everything* sounds pretty comprehensive to me,' said Bram.

'You may mock, but nothing's going right at the moment,' Sophie grumbled. The wind was blowing her curls about her face, and Bram watched her trying to hold them back with one hand. Sophie's hair, he always thought, was a bit like her personality—wildly curling and unruly. Or you might say, as her mother frequently did, that it was messy and out of control.

A lot of people only saw the unruliness—or messiness—and not the softness or the silkiness or the unusual colours. At first glance her hair was a dull brown, but if you looked closely you could see that there were other colours in there too: gold and copper and bronze where it caught the light.

The quirkiness of Sophie's personality was reflected in her face. Vivid, rather than strictly pretty, it was dominated by a pair of bright eyes that were an unusual shade somewhere between grey and green. They made Bram think of a river, ever-changing with the light and the flow of the water. She had a wide, mobile mouth, and a set of the chin that revealed the stubbornness that had led to constant battles with her conventional mother as she was growing up.

'I'm a big fat failure on every front,' Sophie was saying, unaware of his scrutiny. 'I'm thirty-one,' she began, counting her problems off on her fingers, 'I'm living in a grotty rented flat in a place I don't want to be, and I'm about to lose my job—so chances are that I won't even be able to pay for that any more. I've already lost the love of my life, and my ambitions for a glittering career as a potter have gone down the pan as well, since the only gallery I've ever persuaded to show my work has closed.' She sighed. 'Oh, and now I'm being blackmailed!'

Bram raised an eyebrow. 'Sounds bad.'

'Sounds bad?' Sophie echoed, regarding him with a mixture of resentment and resigned affection as he leant steady and solid on the gate beside her. In his filthy trousers, big mud-splattered boots and torn jumper, he looked exactly what he was—a hill farmer with a powerful body and a quiet, ordinary face. 'Is that all you can say?'

'What would you like me to say?' he asked, looking at her with a trace of amusement in his blue eyes.

'Well, you could gasp with horror, for a start,' Sophie told him severely. 'Honestly, anyone would think blackmail was an everyday occurrence on the North Yorkshire moors! You could at least try saying *How dreadful* or *Poor you* or something. Not just *Sounds bad*!'

'Sorry,' said Bram with mock humility. 'I just had this

idea that your mother might be up to her old tricks again.'

He was right, of course. Sophie blew out a long breath. 'How did you guess?' she asked, her voice laced with irony.

It wasn't hard. Harriet Beckwith had emotional blackmail down to a fine art, having honed it over the years as Sophie was growing up.

'What's she up to now?'

'She wants me to come home for Christmas,' said Sophie, wriggling her shoulders against the cold, her expression glum. 'She's got it all planned. We're going to have a jolly family Christmas all together.'

'Ah.' Bram got the problem immediately. 'And Melissa…?'

'Will be there,' Sophie finished for him. She pulled some wayward strands of hair from her mouth, where they were being flattened by the wind. 'With Nick, of course.'

She had made an effort to keep her voice light, but Bram could hear what it cost her just to say her brother-in-law's name.

'Can't you say you're going away with friends, like you did last year? Say you're going skiing or something.'

'I would if I could afford it, but I'm completely broke,' said Sophie morosely. 'I suppose I could pretend that I was going, but then I'd have to spend the whole of Christmas hiding out in my flat and not answering the phone, eking out a tin of sardines and watching jolly Christmas specials until I tried to strangle myself with a piece of tinsel.'

'That doesn't sound like much fun,' said Bram.

'No,' she agreed with another sigh. 'Anyway, it

wouldn't work. Mum's got it all covered. She's reminded me that it's Dad's seventieth birthday on December the twenty-third and she wants to have a family party for him.'

'Hence the emotional blackmail?'

'Exactly.' Sophie put on her mother's voice. '"*It's so long since we've all been together. We never see you any more. It would mean so much to your father.*"' The expressive greeny grey eyes darkened. 'Mum says Dad hasn't been well recently. He told *me* that he was perfectly all right, but you know what Dad's like. He'd say that if he was being hung, drawn and quartered!

'On the other hand, he might be fine. I wouldn't put it past Mum to embellish the fact that he's had a cold or something. She even hinted that the farm was getting too much for them, and that they might have to sell, which would mean that this might be our last Christmas at Glebe Farm.'

Sophie hunched her shoulders in her jacket. 'She didn't try that one in front of Dad! He's always said that the only way he's ever leaving the farm is in a box.'

That sounded more like Joe Beckwith. Bram could see Sophie's difficulty. She had always been very close to her father.

'Tricky,' he commented carefully.

'I feel awful for even hesitating,' Sophie confessed miserably. 'I mean, Dad's never been the touchy-feely type, and he's never cared about birthdays before, but I think this one will be different. I have to be there.'

Bram ruminated, hands clasped lightly together as he leant on the gate. 'Could you be here for the party on the twenty-third and then make plans to go somewhere else for Christmas? At least then you'd only have to coincide for a night.'

'I tried that, but that's when the blackmail really started! Mum said that she would just cancel the whole idea of a party for him if I was going to rush off like that. Was it so much to expect Dad to have a happy birthday and what might be his last Christmas with his family around him? How would I be able to enjoy Christmas knowing that I had been so selfish and hurt my parents and spoilt things for everybody?'

She sighed. 'You can imagine it.'

Bram could. He had known Harriet Beckwith for as long as he could remember. If she had decided that they were going to have a family Christmas, poor Sophie didn't stand a chance.

'Would it be so bad?' he asked gently.

'No, no—probably not. I'm obviously making a big fuss about nothing, the way I always do.' Sophie made a brave attempt at a smile. 'It's just…'

'Seeing Nick again,' Bram finished for her quietly as her voice cracked.

She nodded, her mouth wobbling too much to speak. Biting her lip fiercely, she scowled at the view. 'I ought to be over it,' she burst out after a moment. 'That's what everyone says. It's time to move on. Get over it.'

'It takes time, Sophie,' said Bram. 'Your fiancé left you for your sister. That's not the kind of thing you can get over easily.'

He would never forget her face when she had first told him about Nick. Incandescent with happiness, she had been too excited to stand still.

Throwing her arms out, she had spun round, laughing, alight, radiating joy. 'I am so, so happy!' she had said, and Bram had looked at his childhood friend, scrubby, sturdy Sophie, with her tangled hair and her stubborn streak, and, startled, had seen her transformed.

For years he had hardly thought about her at all. She was just Sophie, just there, part of his life. He had missed her a little when she went away to college, but he'd had other things to distract him. They had caught up whenever she came home, and she'd always been exactly the same turbulent, tomboyish Sophie—his friend. She was funny, warm, chaotic—the kind of girl you could talk to, the kind of girl you laughed with, but not the kind of girl you slept with. Not the kind of girl you even thought about sleeping with.

So, it had been a strange feeling to look at her suddenly in a different light, to see her the same and yet somehow not the same at all.

Sophie had babbled on, too excited to notice the arrested expression in his eyes, or to realise that Bram—unflappable, unshockable Bram—had at last been taken unawares.

'I never knew what walking on air meant until now,' she had told him. 'Oh, Bram, I can't wait for you to meet Nick. He's incredible! He's clever and witty and glamorous and, oh…just *gorgeous*! I can't *believe* he loves me too when he could have anyone he wanted.'

Closing her eyes, she'd hugged herself in remembered ecstasy. 'I have to keep pinching myself to see if I'll wake up and find that it's all just a wonderful dream…and I know that I couldn't bear it if it was. I think I'd die!'

That was his Sophie, Bram remembered thinking affectionately. No half measures for her. He should have guessed that when she fell in love it would be totally, utterly and passionately. Moderation simply wasn't in her vocabulary.

'Nick's asked me to marry him already,' Sophie had said, glowing in that new, unexpectedly disturbing way.

'I haven't said anything to Mum and Dad yet. I know they'd think I haven't known him for very long, and they might think it was a bit soon, but Melissa's going to come and stay with me in London in a couple of weeks, so I thought I could introduce him to the family gradually. I'm sure she'll report back and tell them how fantastic he is, and then it won't be like springing the news on them when I bring him up in a month or so.'

But that wasn't quite how it had worked out.

He had been on his way home at the end of an unusually hot, still day in July when he had spotted a solitary figure trudging across the moor. Stopping the tractor, Bram had waited for her to reach him. He'd known it was Sophie, and he'd known from the brittle way that she held herself that something was very wrong.

Sophie hadn't said a word as she'd come up to him. Bess had greeted her with her usual enthusiasm, and when Sophie had looked up from patting the dog the stricken expression in her eyes had made Bram's heart contract.

Wordlessly, he'd moved to make way for her on the tractor step beside him, and for a while they'd just sat in silence while the evening sun turned the hillsides to gold. It had been very quiet. Bess had panted in the shade beneath the tractor, but otherwise all had been still.

'I always thought it was too good to be true,' Sophie had said eventually. And for Bram the worst thing was hearing her voice. She had always been so fiery, so alive, but now all the emotion seemed to have been emptied out of her, leaving her sounding flat and utterly expressionless. Utterly unlike Sophie.

'Do you want to talk about it?' he asked carefully.

'I shouldn't. I promised that I wouldn't tell anyone,' she said, in the same dull tone.

'What? Even your oldest friend?'

She looked at him then, the river-coloured eyes stark with suffering. 'I think at least you'd understand,' she said.

'Then tell me,' said Bram. 'Is it Nick?'

Sophie nodded dully. 'He doesn't love me any more.'

'What happened?'

'He saw Melissa. He took one look at her and fell out of love with me and in love with her. I saw it happen,' she said, in that terrible, brittle voice. 'I watched his face and I knew that was it.'

Bram didn't know what to say. 'Oh, Sophie…'

'I should have expected it,' she said, not looking at him. 'You know what Melissa is like.'

Bram did know. Sophie's sister was the most beautiful girl he had ever seen. She had an ethereal golden love-liness that was somehow out of place on the Yorkshire moors, unlike Sophie's vibrant sturdiness.

It was hard to believe that the two were sisters. Melissa was nothing like Sophie. She was sweet and fragile and helpless, and few men were immune to her appeal. Bram certainly wasn't. Sometimes it seemed to him that their brief engagement ten years ago was no more than a dream. How could a practical, ordinary man like him ever have hoped to hold on to such a treasure?

Bram couldn't in all honesty blame Nick for falling for Melissa, but he hated him for hurting Sophie.

'What did you do?'

'What could I do? There was no point in pretending that nothing had happened. When we got back that night I gave him back his ring. I told him there was no point in all three of us being unhappy.' Sophie smiled a little bitterly. 'I let him go. Ella said that I should have fought to keep him, but how could I compete with Melissa?'

'He might have forgotten her when she left,' Bram suggested. He had noticed that about Melissa himself. When she was there, it was impossible to look at anyone else, but once she had gone it was sometimes hard to remember exactly what she was like, or what she had said, or how he had felt—other than dazzled by her sweetness and her beauty.

Sophie wasn't like that, he realised with something like surprise. She wasn't beautiful as Melissa was beautiful, but he kept a vivid picture of her in his mind, of her expressions and her laughter and the way she waved her hands around as she talked. He could always picture Sophie exactly.

'He might have forgotten her,' Sophie agreed, 'and I might have tried harder if it hadn't been for Melissa. I saw her face too. You know she's used to men being in love with her, but I don't think that she's ever really been in love herself before.'

She stopped abruptly, remembering too late that Bram had loved Melissa for a very long time. The last thing she wanted to do was hurt Bram. 'Sorry,' she said, contrite.

'It's OK,' said Bram. 'I know what you mean.' Sophie was right. Melissa was more used to being loved than to loving. It was just the way things were when you looked the way she did.

'I think that Melissa fell in love for the first time when she saw Nick,' Sophie was saying. 'She looked completely bowled over. She couldn't take her eyes off him, and although she tried not to show it, for my sake, I could see how she felt. Who could understand better than me?' she added, with a brave attempt at a wry smile.

'It was too late for me,' she went on. 'I knew that once Nick had seen her he wouldn't be able to look at me in the same way. If I tried to pretend that nothing has happened it would just make three of us unhappy. At least this way Melissa and Nick have a chance at happiness.'

'Does Melissa know what you've done for her?' asked Bram, thinking that few sisters would have made the sacrifice Sophie had done.

Sophie nodded. 'She felt absolutely awful. She cried when I told her that I wasn't going to marry Nick after all. She said she couldn't do that to me. But I told her that she didn't do anything. It wasn't her fault. She couldn't help falling in love with Nick, and he couldn't help falling in love with her. That's just how it was.'

'So Nick and Melissa are now together?'

'Yes.' Sophie looked down at her hands and fought to get the words past the terrible tightness in her throat. She wouldn't cry any more, she *wouldn't*. 'Nick's moved up to join Melissa here, and they're going to set up an outdoor clothing business together. They're getting married in September.' There—the hardest bit was out. 'That's why I'm back now. Mum wants me to try on my bridesmaid's dress.'

'You're going to be Melissa's *bridesmaid*?' Bram said incredulously. 'Sophie, surely you don't have to put yourself through that? It's asking too much of you.'

'It would look odd if I wasn't her bridesmaid,' she tried to explain. 'My parents don't know about me and Nick. I thought it would make them feel awkward. They wouldn't know how to treat him if they knew what had happened, so I suggested to Melissa that we didn't tell them.

'As far as they're concerned Melissa met him in London when she came to visit me. Then my fiancé dumped me at around the same time and was, coincidentally, also called Nick. At least that will explain why I'm not on very good form at the moment.' She managed a twisted smile. 'Mum thinks I'm jealous because Melissa's getting married and I'm not.'

Bram's brows drew together. 'That's not very fair on you.'

Sophie shrugged. 'To be honest, I feel so dead inside I don't care. Melissa and Nick have got a life to build up here. There's no point in making things difficult for them, or for Mum and Dad, who'll see them all the time. I think it's better for everyone if only Nick and Melissa and I know what really happened. I promised I wouldn't tell anyone else.

'I shouldn't really have told you,' she said rather helplessly. 'It's just…sometimes I feel so alone,' she burst out. 'I feel so wretched and miserable and lonely, and I hate myself for not being able to snap out of it. I'm spoiling Melissa's wedding, as Mum keeps pointing out, but there's no one for me to talk to,' she said, her voice wobbling treacherously. 'I can't talk to Melissa because she'll just feel even more guilty that I'm so upset, and no one else knows the truth.'

Bram put his arm around her shoulders and pulled her against him, feeling how rigidly she was holding herself as she struggled for control. 'I know the truth now,' he said. 'I'm glad you told me. You can talk to me whenever you want.'

The urge to burst into tears and sob out all her pain and misery onto his broad shoulder was so strong that

Sophie had to struggle for long moments before she could straighten and muster a wavery smile.

'Thanks, Bram,' she said. 'I feel better already for having told you.'

His arm fell from her shoulder. 'What can I do?' he asked simply.

Sophie hesitated. 'Would you...would you come to the wedding? I know it will be hard for you to watch Melissa getting married, Bram, and I feel bad about asking you, but it would mean a lot for me to know that there was someone there for me.'

So Bram had gone to the wedding. Of course he had done it for Sophie. He had stood in the village church and watched Melissa, looking more beautiful than ever, her lovely face lifted adoringly to Nick, and strangely it hadn't hurt as much as he had thought it would.

Perhaps he had been too worried about Sophie to think too much about his own feelings. Bram didn't know how she had held herself together through the wedding. She had smiled and chatted, and Bram had wondered if he was only one who could see the agony in her eyes, the only one who knew how much it had cost her to play her part, the only one who appreciated how brave she was.

Sophie had waved her sister off on her honeymoon with the man she herself loved, and gone back to London. She hadn't seen them since, and only came home to the moors when she knew they were away. She made excuses to her parents, but Bram knew it was because of Nick.

Tucking her hand into his arm, Sophie brought him back to the raw November present, and as she leant companionably against his shoulder Bram was conscious of being aware of her in a way that he hadn't noticed before. He'd never realised how soft she felt, or how well she fitted into the curve of his body.

She was just the right height, too. He'd never noticed that before either. Her tousled curls tickled his chin softly. They smelt clean and fresh, with the coconutty whiff of gorse flowers.

Of course the shampoo might have been meant to smell of coconuts themselves, Bram acknowledged, in an attempt to distract himself from the feel of Sophie's body pressed into him, but he was more of a gorse man himself. He had never lain on a tropical beach under a leaning coconut palm and he didn't want to. Give him a hillside and a gorse bush in bloom any day. The bright, brave yellow flowers, with their slightly exotic fragrance, and the sturdy spikiness of the gorse reminded him of Sophie.

'It's been over a year,' she was saying, unaware of his uneasy distraction. 'I thought I would be starting to forget Nick now, but I think I still love him just as much as I did when we were engaged. I've never felt like that about anyone before, and I can't imagine ever loving anyone else in the same way. I just don't see how I'll ever get over him.'

'Was he so perfect?' Bram asked. He had met Nick briefly at the wedding, and he hadn't been that impressed. Melissa's husband had struck him as patronising and more than a little smug—but then he would probably have felt smug if he'd won Melissa, Bram had to acknowledge.

'No, Nick's not perfect,' said Sophie. 'He can be arrogant sometimes, and I think he's a bit self-centred, but there was just something so exciting about him... I don't know. It's chemistry, I suppose. I can't really explain how he made me feel. And now I can't bear the thought of another man touching me.'

Bram wasn't quite sure how he felt about hearing that, especially when her soft warmth was leaning against him and he was wondering, bizarrely, what it would feel like to put his arm round her and pull her closer.

'I've tried to meet other men,' Sophie continued, 'but I just end up remembering how it was with Nick. I tell myself that it would be different if I actually came face to face with him again, but I'm afraid. What if it isn't different? What if it's exactly the same? Melissa would see that I still loved him, and that would just make things worse for her.'

'Is that why you stay in London?'

She nodded. 'I don't like it there, and I'm desperately homesick, but if I came home I'd have to see Nick all the time, and I don't know how I'd bear that. Melissa feels terrible about it all. She rings me sometimes and begs me to come up and see them, but I can't face it, and then *I* feel awful for upsetting her.

'It might be different if I had a boyfriend, someone to make Melissa—and Nick, I suppose—think that I was over it and had moved on, but I can't produce a man out of nowhere! My mother thinks it's all my fault. She's dying to get me married.'

'Why?' asked Bram, baffled.

'Oh, because she loved Melissa's wedding and can't wait to organise another one. She was very put out when Susan Jackson got married last summer. You know what rivals she is with Maggie Jackson! Mum was really cross that Maggie had managed to marry off no less than three daughters, *and* all with what Mum calls ''proper weddings'', in a church, with long white dresses and a marquee in the garden!'

Sophie shook her head ruefully. 'I get the definite feeling that I'm letting the side down. Mum's got this idea that if I'd only make the effort to lose some weight and smarten myself up a bit I'd be able to snaffle up a husband in no time! She's always asking me if I've met *anyone nice.*'

'What do you say?'

'I suppose I play along with it a bit, just for a quiet life,' said Sophie a little uncomfortably. 'If I'm seeing someone I let Mum think that it's more serious than it is. I went out with a guy called Rob for a while, and she got very excited about him. He's a teacher, and she thought he sounded very suitable, but I had to tell her today that I'm not seeing him any more. That didn't go down very well.'

She pushed the hair out of her eyes and managed a smile. 'Mum thinks I'm *"just not trying"*!'

Bram could practically hear Harriet Beckwith saying it.

'The thing is, Rob's a nice guy, but...'

'But he's not Nick?'

'No,' she acknowledged with a sigh. 'No, he isn't. The trouble is that nobody is ever going to be Nick, but I can't tell Mum that. She got all upset because she was hoping I'd bring Rob home for Christmas, and of course now she wants to know why it's all over.'

'What did you tell her?'

Sophie grimaced, remembering. 'Well, I didn't know what to say, so I said I'd fallen in love with someone else but it was all very new and I didn't really want to talk about it yet. It was the best I could think of on the spur of the moment,' she added defensively, as if Bram had poured scorn on her idea.

'But of course now Mum's in full interrogation mode.

She keeps accusing me of being secretive and difficult. Why can't I be sweet and nice like Melissa, who keeps in touch and goes to see them all the time? We ended up having a full-scale row, and I stormed out. It was just like being a teenager again.' She sighed.

And, just like then, she had sought refuge at Haw Gill Farm. Straightening from the comfort of his warm bulk, Sophie looked at Bram and wondered if he had any idea how much he meant to her. He was such a dear friend, so level-headed, so down to earth, so reassuringly solid. The mere sight of him was enough to make her feel safer and steadier.

'All I could think of was coming to see you,' she said simply.

CHAPTER TWO

BRAM'S side felt cold where Sophie had been leaning against him, and part of him wished that she would come back, instead of turning up her collar against the cold and thrusting her hands into her pockets like that. The other part of him was glad that she had moved away. For some reason her nearness was making him feel strange today.

So strange that when Bess, snuffling along the hedgerow, put up a pheasant, he actually jumped as it exploded out of its hiding place, squawking with indignation.

It made Sophie start, too, and she looked guiltily at the bales still waiting to be unloaded in the fading light of the winter afternoon.

'I'm sorry,' she said. 'I've held you up. You've got better things to do than listen to me moaning on.'

'You know I always enjoy listening to you moan,' said Bram lightly, 'but I should finish moving those bales.' He glanced down at Sophie. 'It won't take long. Why don't you go and put the kettle on? You know what Mum used to say...'

'It'll all feel better after a nice cup of tea!' she chanted obediently.

Molly Thoresby had been a great believer in the power of tea. How many times had Sophie heard her say that? She smiled at the memory as she walked back to the farmhouse. She could see Molly now, lifting the lid on the old kitchen range, setting the kettle firmly on the

23

stove, while Sophie sat at the table and poured out her problems.

Sophie loved her own mother, of course she did, but she had loved Bram's almost as much. Harriet Beckwith was smart and well-groomed, while Molly had been warm and comfortable and wise. Molly had never pushed or criticised or complained the way Harriet did. She'd just listened and made tea, and funnily enough things almost always *had* felt better afterwards. When Molly had died suddenly, a couple of months ago, Sophie had felt nearly as bereft as Bram.

The big farmhouse kitchen looked exactly the same as it had always done, with its sturdy pine table set in the window, its cluttered dresser and the two shabby armchairs drawn up in front of a wood-burning stove, but it was empty without Molly.

The clock on the mantelpiece ticked into the silence. Sophie filled the kettle and set it to boil on the range, just the way Molly had used to do. She had always loved this shabby, comfortable kitchen. Her mother's was immaculate, full of modern appliances and spacious work surfaces, but it wasn't a place you wanted to linger.

Outside, the sky was streaked with pink over the moors, and it was getting darker by the minute. Sophie liked the short winter afternoons, and the way switching on a lamp could make the darkness beyond the windows intensify. She put on the lights in the kitchen so that Bram could see their inviting yellow glow as he came home. It must be awful for him coming back to a dark house each evening now that Molly had gone.

She stood in the big bay window and watched the light fade over the moors. Her mind drifted to thoughts of Nick, the way it always did at quiet times like this. She thought about his heart-shaking smile, about the shiver of pleasure that went through her at the merest brush of his fingers, about the thrill of being near him.

Being with Nick had never felt safe—not in the way being with Bram did, for instance. There had always been an element of risk in their relationship. Sophie could see that now. She had never been able to relax completely with Nick for fear that she would lose him. Even when she had been at her happiest it had felt as if she were on point of exploding with the sheer intensity of it all. It had been a dangerous feeling, but a wonderful one too. Loving Nick had made her feel electric, *alive*.

Would she ever feel that way again? Sophie wondered. It didn't seem possible. There was only one Nick, and he belonged to her sister now.

The sound of the back door opening jerked Sophie out of her thoughts.

'In your kennel, Bess,' she heard Bram say. 'Stay!'

Poor old Bess was a softie amongst sheepdogs. Sophie was sure that she secretly yearned to be a pet, so that she could come inside and sit by the fire. Every day she sat hopefully at the door while Bram took his boots off, before being ordered off to her warm, clean kennel.

'You're a working dog,' Bram would tell her sternly. 'You can come in when you retire.'

'That dog is hopeless,' he said as he came into the kitchen wearing thick grey socks on his feet. His brown hair was ruffled by the wind, and his eyes looked so blue in his square, brown face that for a startled moment Sophie felt as if she were looking at a stranger.

'She's not that bad,' said Sophie as she warmed the teapot.

'She is. She's useless. I'm never going have a starring role on *One Man and His Dog* with Bess.' Bram pretended to complain. 'Sometimes I think it would be easier to run around after the sheep myself and let Bess have the whistle!'

Sophie laughed. 'At least she tries. And she adores you.'

'I wish she'd adore me by doing what I told her,' sighed Bram.

'I'm afraid that's not how adoring works,' said Sophie sadly, and he glanced at her, compassion in his blue eyes.

'No,' he said. 'I know.'

Sophie kept swirling the hot water around in the teapot.

'Does it ever get any better, Bram?' she asked.

He didn't pretend not to understand her. 'Yes, it does,' he said. 'Eventually.'

'It doesn't seem to have got better with you,' she pointed out. 'How long is it since you were engaged to Melissa?'

'More than ten years,' he admitted.

'And you're still not totally over her, are you?'

Bram didn't answer immediately. He warmed his hands by the wood-burning stove and thought about Melissa, with her hair like spun gold and her violet eyes and that smile that made the sun come out.

'I am over her,' he said, although he didn't sound that convincing even to himself. 'I don't hurt the way I used to. It's true that I think about her sometimes, though. I think about what it would have been like if she hadn't broken our engagement, but it's hard to imagine now. Would Melissa have been a good farmer's wife?'

Probably not, Sophie thought. In spite of growing up on a farm, Melissa had never been a great one for getting her hands dirty. She had never needed to. She'd always seemed so helpless and fragile that there had always been someone to do the dirty jobs for her.

Sophie had long ago accepted that she would have to get on and do things that Melissa would never have to contemplate, but she didn't feel resentful about it. She loved her sister, and was proud of her beauty. When they were younger she had used to roll her eyes and call Melissa the sister from hell, but she hadn't really minded.

Until Nick.

'I do still love Melissa,' said Bram. 'Part of me always will. But I don't feel raw, the way you do at the moment, Sophie. I know it's a terrible cliché, but time really does heal.'

The pot was as warm as it was ever going to be. Sophie threw the water away, dropped in a couple of teabags and poured in boiling water from the kettle.

'Is Melissa the reason you've never married?' she asked, setting the pot on the table.

Bram pulled out a chair and sat down. 'Partly,' he conceded. 'But it's not as if I'm still waiting for her or anything. I'm ready to find someone else.'

'I thought Rachel was good for you,' volunteered Sophie. 'I really liked her.'

If anyone could have helped him get over Melissa, Sophie would have thought it would be Rachel. She was a solicitor in Helmsley, warm and funny and intelligent and stylish. And practical. Bram needed someone practical.

'I liked her too,' said Bram. 'She was great. I thought we might be able to make a go of it, but it turned out that we wanted very different things. Rachel wasn't cut out to be a farmer's wife. She told me quite frankly that she didn't think she could stick the isolation, and the moors frightened her in the dark. She wanted to move to York, where she could go out in the evenings, meet friends for a drink, watch a film…and I couldn't stick living in the city.'

He shrugged. 'So we decided to call it a day.'

'I'm sorry,' said Sophie, wondering if Rachel might not have realised that a big part of Bram's heart would always be Melissa's. Even if she had never met Nick, she didn't think that she would have wanted to marry someone who was still in love with another woman.

From sheer force of habit she went over to the dresser, where Molly had always kept a battered tin commemorating the Queen's wedding. Inside there would be a mouth-watering selection of homemade biscuits—things like flapjacks or rock cakes or coconut slices. But when Sophie pulled off the lid it was empty.

Of course it was. Stupid, she chided herself. When would Bram have had time to do any baking?

Nothing could have brought home more clearly that Molly was gone. Sophie bit her lip and replaced the lid carefully.

'I miss your mum,' she said.

'I know. I miss her too.' Bram got up and found a packet of biscuits in the larder. 'We'd better put them on her special plate,' he said, taking it down from the dresser. 'She wouldn't like the way standards have slipped around here!'

Sophie had made Molly the plate for Christmas, the first year that she had discovered the pleasure of clay between her hands. She had fired it and then painted it herself with some rather wobbly sheep. Compared to her later work the plate was laughably crude, but Molly had been delighted, and had insisted on using it every time they had tea.

Bram shook the biscuits onto the plate and put it on the table. Then he sat down again opposite Sophie and watched her pour tea into two mugs.

'It was funny coming back to the house tonight,' he said. 'The lights were on, and I could hear the kettle whistling…it was almost as if Mum was still here. This is when I miss her most, when I come in at night to an empty house. She was always here…cooking, listening to the radio, drinking tea… It's as if she's just popped out to feed the chickens or get something from larder. I keep thinking that she'll walk back in any minute.'

Sophie's eyes filled with tears. 'Oh, Bram, I'm so sorry. I go on and on about my own problems, but losing Molly was much, much worse than anything I've had to deal with. How are you coping?'

'Oh, I'm fine,' said Bram easily, as she had known that he would. 'It's only now that I understand how much Mum did for me, though. When she was around I didn't really have to think about cooking or shopping or washing. I guess I was spoilt.'

'Are you eating properly?' Sophie asked, knowing that Molly would have wanted her to check.

He nodded. 'I can't manage anything very posh, and I'm always forgetting to go to the shops, but I won't starve. It's not that I can't look after myself, but there seem to be so many household chores I never knew about before, and it all takes so much time when I get in at night.'

'Welcome to the world of women,' said Sophie dryly, taking a biscuit and pushing the plate towards him.

'Sorry.' Bram grimaced an apology. 'That sounded as if I was looking for a replacement servant, didn't it? It's not that,' he said. 'I just wish I had known how hard Mum worked when she was alive. I wish I hadn't taken it all for granted, and that I could have told her how much I appreciated everything that she did for me.'

Sophie's heart ached for him. 'Molly loved you,' she told him. 'And she knew you loved her. You didn't need to tell her anything.'

Bram helped himself to sugar and sat stirring his tea abstractedly. 'I don't know how I'm going to manage when it comes to lambing,' he confessed. 'You need at least two of you then.'

Lambing time would be the hardest. Sophie had grown up on a farm and she knew how carefully the farmers watched their sheep, all day and all night, desperate to ensure that as many lambs as possible survived.

She always quite liked helping with the lambing herself. She loved the smell of hay and the bleating sheep and the way the tiniest of lambs staggered to their feet to find their mothers. But she only did it for the occasional night. She didn't have to spend three weeks or more with barely a chance of sleep. There were plenty of other times, too, when a farmer like Bram really did need help.

'It's hard running a farm on your own,' she said, and he sighed at little.

'I see now why Mum was so keen for me to get married.' He stirred his tea some more. 'I've been thinking about it a lot since she died,' he admitted after a while. 'As long as Mum was alive I didn't need to face up to the fact that I'd lost Melissa.' He paused, listening to his own words, and frowned. 'Does that make sense?' he asked Sophie.

'You mean it was easy to use Melissa as an excuse for why it never quite worked out with anyone else?'

Bram looked rueful. 'It doesn't sound very good when you put it like that, does it? But I think that's what I did, in a way. None of my other girlfriends ever made me feel the way Melissa did, and I suppose I didn't need to try while Mum was here and everything carried on as normal.

'Now she's dead...' He trailed off for a moment, trying to explain. 'I get lonely sometimes,' he admitted at last. 'I sit here in the evenings and think about what my life is going to be like if I don't get married, and I don't like it. I think it's time I put Melissa behind me for good. I've got to stop comparing every woman I meet to her and move on properly.'

'Moving on is easier said than done,' Sophie pointed out, thinking of Nick, and Bram smiled in rueful agreement.

'Especially when you live up on the moors and spend whole days when you only get to meet sheep and talk to Bess. It's not that easy to find a girl you want to marry at the best of times, and it seems to me that the older you get, the harder it is.'

Sophie thought about it. For the first time it occurred to her that there weren't a lot of opportunities to meet people up here. There was the pub in the village, of course, but the community was small and it wasn't often that newcomers moved into the area. Those who did tended to like the idea of country life without actually wanting to live it twenty-four hours a day. Most used their cottages as weekend retreats, or commuted into town.

Maybe it *wasn't* that easy for Bram. You would think it would be easy for a single, solvent, steady man in his early thirties to find a girlfriend, thought Sophie, remembering the complaints of her single friends in London. They were always moaning that all the decent men were already married. Bram might not be classically handsome, but he was kind and decent and utterly reliable. He would make someone a very good husband.

'You should come to London,' she said. 'You'd be snapped up.'

'Not much point if the woman doing the snapping doesn't fancy the idea of life on an isolated farm,' said Bram. 'A girl who's squeamish and hates cold mornings and mud is no good to me. That's obviously where I've been going wrong all these years. When I think about it, since Melissa all my girlfriends have been town girls at heart, which means that I've been looking in the wrong place. What I need is a country girl.'

Sophie looked at him affectionately. Yes, a nice country girl was exactly what Bram needed. Surely there was someone out there who would be glad to make a life with Bram? She would have this lovely kitchen to cook in, and on winter nights she could draw the thick, faded red curtains in the sitting room against the wind and the rain and sit with Bram in front of the fire, listening to it spit and crackle.

'I wish I could marry you,' she said with a wistful smile.

Bram put down his mug. His mother's clock ticked into the sudden silence.

'Why don't you?' he said.

Sophie smiled a little uncertainly. He was joking, wasn't he? 'Why don't I marry you?' she echoed doubtfully, just to check.

'You just said that you wished you could,' Bram reminded her.

'I know I *said* that, but I meant…' Sophie was so thrown by the apparent seriousness in his face that she couldn't now remember what she had meant. 'I didn't mean that we should actually get married,' she tried to explain.

'Why not?'

Her wary look deepened. What was going on? 'Well, it's obvious, isn't it?' she said, puzzled. 'We don't love each other.'

'I love you,' said Bram, calmly drinking his tea.

'And I love you,' she hastened to reassure him. 'But it's not the same.' She struggled to find the right words. 'It's not the way you should love someone when you get married.'

'You mean you don't love me the way you love Nick?'

Sophie flushed slightly. 'Yes. Or the way you love Melissa. It's different; you know it is. We're friends, not lovers.'

'That's why it could work,' said Bram. 'We're both in the same position, so we understand how each other feels.'

He paused, trying to work it out in his mind. It had never occurred to him even to think about marrying Sophie before, but now that it had the idea seemed obvious. Why hadn't he thought of it before?

'If neither of us can have the person we really want, we could at least have each other.' He tried to convince her. 'It wouldn't be like taking a risk on a stranger. We've known each other all our lives. You know what I'm like, and I know you. I'm not going to run away appalled when I discover all your irritating habits the way a stranger might do.'

Sophie paused in the middle of dunking a biscuit in her tea. '*What* irritating habits?' she demanded.

'Irritating was the wrong word,' Bram corrected himself, perceiving that he was straying onto dangerous ground. 'I should have said that I know your...quirks.'

She wasn't going to let it go that easily! 'Like what?'

'Like the way you screw up your face when you're trying to decide what you want to drink in the pub. The way you always say that you don't want any crisps and then eat all of mine.' He paused to think. 'Those funny earrings you wear sometimes.'

Her mouth full of biscuit, Sophie put her hands up to her ears in an instinctively defensive gesture. Her friend Ella was a jewellery designer, and made all her earrings for her now. 'What's funny about them?'

Bram studied the feathery drops that trembled from her lobes. They were relatively restrained compared to the weird shapes and colours she usually wore. 'You've got to admit they're pretty unusual,' he said.

Sophie sniffed and reached for another biscuit. 'Anything else?'

'Well, there's the way you eat your way through a whole packet of biscuits and then spend the rest of the evening complaining that you feel fat,' said Bram.

Freezing with the biscuit halfway to her mouth, Sophie saw too late that he was teasing. 'Don't you want to know what *your* irritating habits are?'

'Tell me the worst,' he invited.

'You're infuriatingly calm. You never make a fuss. You never get carried away.' Sophie ate the biscuit anyway, with a certain defiance. 'I can't imagine a situation in which you'd lose your cool.'

Bram looked at her. 'Can't you?'

There was a tiny pause, and for some reason Sophie found herself picturing Bram making love with a vividness that was startling and more than a little disturbing in its clarity. He would be slow and sure to start with, but as the excitement built—yes, he might lose his cool then...

To her horror, Sophie realised that she was blushing. It didn't seem right to be thinking of Bram in that way. She took another biscuit to give herself something to do.

'OK, I'll admit your habits aren't as irritating as mine,' she said, after a moment.

'As irritating habits go, ours aren't incompatible, though, are they?'

There was another pause while Sophie eyed Bram, still half convinced that he was joking. 'You're not thinking about this idea seriously, are you?'

Bram was turning his mug between square, capable hands, studying it thoughtfully. 'I might be.'

His eyes lifted to her face once more, suddenly very blue and keen. 'Why don't we face reality, Sophie? Neither of us has got a chance of marrying the person we love. We can live alone and miserable, or we can live together. Our marriage might not be one of grand passion, but we would have friendship, companionship, comfort. They count for something.

'I need help on the farm, to put it bluntly,' he went on. 'Sophie, I'd love to have you as my wife. I need someone who understands the moors and isn't afraid of being up here on her own—someone who can help me run the place. A partner as well as a wife. Someone just like you. And you...you can't have what you really want either, but you did say you wanted to come home. You've always loved it here. Well, you could live here all the time with me. Haw Gill Farm would be your home as well as mine. You could set up a wheel and a kiln in one of the barns and start potting again.'

The blue eyes rested on Sophie's face. 'Neither of us would have everything we wanted, but we would have some of it. Perfect happy-ever-after endings are for books and films, Sophie. We wouldn't be the first people to compromise, to settle for good enough rather than the best.'

'Compromising means giving up on your dreams,' Sophie pointed out.

'It means having something instead of nothing,' countered Bram. 'And it would solve your Christmas problem if nothing else,' he added cunningly. 'You said yourself that it would be easier to get through a family Christmas if you could produce a boyfriend. Why shouldn't that boyfriend be me?'

'Well…because they all know you,' she said.

'So?'

'They know we've been friends all our lives. It doesn't seem very likely that we'd suddenly decide to fall in love. Anyway,' she remembered, 'I've already told Mum that I'm in love with someone else.'

'You didn't say who it was, though,' he reminded her. 'Why couldn't it be me?'

'Because I would have told her if it had been you,' said Sophie, a little baffled by his persistence and still more than half convinced that he was joking.

'Not necessarily. If we'd only just realised that we were in love ourselves, I think we'd want a little time to get used to the idea before we told everybody. We wouldn't rush out and spread the news straight away, would we?'

Sophie looked sceptical. 'So we'd ask Mum and Dad and everyone else to believe that after all these years of being friends we suddenly looked at each other and fell in love?'

Bram shrugged. 'It happens. I think it's possible to

look at someone familiar and suddenly see them in a completely different light.'

He remembered how startled he had been to realise how much she had changed when she was telling him about falling in love with Nick. Of course that wasn't the same as falling in love with her, but still, it had been a shock. And look how conscious he had been of her leaning against him by the gate.

'People change,' he said. 'Sometimes when you least expect it.'

'I suppose so,' said Sophie doubtfully. 'I can't really imagine falling in love like that.'

What would it be like? She couldn't imagine it. With Nick it had been love at first sight. One look and she had tumbled helplessly in love with him. How could it be the same if you had known the other person all your life?

Imagine falling in love with Bram, for instance. How weird would that be? Her eyes rested on him speculatively. He had all the right bits, all in the right working order, but they looked exactly the same as they had always done. Eyes, nose, mouth—nothing wrong with any of them, but nothing special either. Nothing to make you stop and think *Hello?*

Although, to be fair, she had always loved Bram's eyes. They were the deep, clear blue of a summer sea, and they gleamed with understated humour.

And actually, now that she looked at him properly, he *did* have rather an intriguing mouth. Funny that she had never noticed that before, thought Sophie. It must be something to do with all this talk about falling in love. She couldn't remember ever noticing Bram's mouth before. It was cool and quiet, as you might expect, but there was something about it that made her feel vaguely…what was the word? Not excited. Not definitely not that. No, disturbed. Did it make her feel just a tiny bit *unsettled*?

Just the teensiest bit sexy?

Horrified by the thought, Sophie shook the feeling aside. This was *Bram*. It felt all wrong to be studying him like this. She shouldn't be thinking about his eyes, and definitely not about his mouth. Not that way, anyway.

'If we were engaged you'd have the perfect excuse to stay here with me rather than at Glebe Farm at Christmas.' Bram returned to the point of the discussion. 'You'd still have to face Nick, of course, on your father's birthday and at Christmas lunch, but it wouldn't be for long. You'd be able to leave whenever you wanted, instead of having to wait for them to decide to go. We can always say that there's a crisis here. We're never short of those,' he added, with a gleam of humour.

It *would* be easier to get through Christmas if Bram were there, Sophie had to admit. He had a quiet self-assurance that lent him an impressive manner. Bram was never rude, never showed off and, more importantly, he never let Sophie's mother rile him. You could always rely on him to ease an awkward silence or defuse tension with humour—qualities which were likely to come in very handy indeed at the Beckwiths' Christmas dinner.

His presence might make things easier for Melissa, too. Sophie was very conscious of how guilty her sister felt about the situation. Perhaps if Melissa thought that she had found happiness with Bram she would be able to relax and enjoy being married to Nick.

And Nick? How would he feel? Would he be glad to think that Sophie had found someone else and was finally over him?

No prizes for guessing how her mother would feel if she and Bram announced their engagement. Harriet would be delighted. Not only would she get the family Christmas she had planned, but she would have another wedding to plan in the New Year. It would be the best Christmas present Sophie could possibly give her.

Her father would be pleased, too, to have both his daughters at his seventieth birthday party.

Yes, it would be easier for everyone if she said that she was marrying Bram.

But could she marry him just to make her family happy?

Sophie turned the mug of tea between her hands.

Could it work? What would it be like to marry Bram? She had never thought of him as anything other than a friend before. What would he be like a husband? As a lover?

She studied him from under her lashes. His mouth was firm, cool, quiet. How would it feel against her own? What would his kiss be like? And those square, capable farmer's hands. She had seen them gently easing a lamb into the world, running assessingly down the flank of a heifer, fixing an engine with deft fingers. She had never felt them smoothing over her skin. What would *that* be like?

The very thought made her uncomfortable.

'This is crazy,' she said, embarrassed. 'I can't believe we're seriously talking about getting married just to save a bit of awkwardness at the Christmas dinner table!'

'I was thinking more about saving awkwardness in life generally,' said Bram lightly, sensing that the moment had gone.

'We could never go through with it,' Sophie said, still torn.

'Couldn't we?'

'No.' Her tentative smile faded. 'No, we couldn't. It's not that I can't see the advantages, Bram. I don't really want to go through life on my own, watching from the sidelines and wasting my time feeling bitter. Of course I don't. But it wouldn't be fair. I care about you too much to marry you knowing how I still feel about Nick. You deserve better than that.'

'Better in what way?' he asked wryly, surprised at the strength of his disappointment.

It was funny. An hour ago the thought of marrying Sophie would never have crossed his mind, but now that it had it seemed like one of the best ideas he had ever had.

'You deserve more than second best, Bram,' said Sophie in a gentle voice. 'You deserve someone who believes in you and loves you completely for yourself, and I know that you'll meet her sooner or later. She'll be real and warm and kind, and you'll wonder how you could ever have loved anyone else. You'll be her rock, and she'll be your star, and you'll be so happy together that you'll wake every morning with her and be grateful to me for not marrying you now.'

Getting up, she moved round the table until she could put her arms around him from behind and bend to kiss his cheek. 'You're my best friend,' she whispered in his ear, and Bram closed his eyes briefly, shocked at the jolt of awareness he felt at her nearness and her warmth.

'I know you're just trying to find a way out for me, but you've got to think of yourself too. I just wish things could be different for both of us.'

Bram put his hand up to cover hers, where they were linked on his chest, and wished that his throat didn't suddenly feel so tight and uncomfortable.

'So do I,' he said.

CHAPTER THREE

HARRIET BECKWITH came out of the kitchen the moment she heard Sophie let herself in at the front door. In spite of wearing an apron and actually holding a rolling pin, she managed to look the antithesis of the clichéd farmer's wife. No buxom figure or floury hands for Sophie's mother. Instead she was a handsome, well-groomed woman, with every hair perfectly in place and an air of brisk competence.

'Look at the state of you, Sophie!' She tutted as Sophie took off her jacket. 'You're absolutely covered in mud! And as for your hair…' She trailed off in despair. 'I suppose you've been up at Haw Gill?'

As always, she managed to make Sophie feel like a scrubby, rather exasperating schoolgirl. Sophie tried not to feel sullen and defensive in response, but it was hard sometimes to remember that she was thirty-one and not fourteen.

'I thought I'd go and see Bram,' she said placatingly.

'I don't know what on earth you two find to talk about,' said Harriet, shaking her head.

What would her mother say if she knew they had been talking about marriage? Sophie watched Harriet pick up the jacket she had just slung carelessly over the chair and brush it down fussily.

Knowing her mother, she'd probably just sigh and say, *Not with your hair like that*, surely, *Sophie?*

'Oh, you know—this and that,' she answered vaguely.

Harriet was still brushing fastidiously. 'Where *have*

you been in this jacket? It's covered in dog hairs and leaves!'

'That'll be from the Land Rover,' said Sophie. 'Bram drove me home.'

They had talked easily enough once they had dropped the bizarre marriage idea. Bram hadn't tried to persuade her to change her mind, and Sophie thought that it was just as well. She had been perilously close to taking him up on his offer at one point, and, even though she was sure that she had made the right decision, she had a nasty feeling that it wouldn't have taken much for her to give in.

It was all just the same as ever. Or almost. Sophie had been aware of a faint constraint on the drive down to Glebe Farm. 'I'll maybe see you at Christmas, then,' was all Bram had said when he dropped her off. He hadn't asked her to think about marrying him, to take her time and maybe reconsider.

So that was that.

'I'm glad to hear that Bram didn't let you go wandering around in the dark,' sniffed Harriet. 'At least *he's* got some sense.'

Bram was always sensible, always practical. Which made it all the more amazing that he would come up with that idea of getting married. He had even managed to make it sound like the obvious solution.

'It's only half past six,' Sophie protested, following her mother into the kitchen as she tried to shake the whole thought of that strange proposal from her mind.

The kitchen at Glebe Farm could not have been more different from the one at Haw Gill. In place of comfortable, shabby chairs and cluttered dressers there were gleaming steel surfaces, installed when Harriet's catering business had begun to take off. That had now been expanded into a specially designed outbuilding, where Sophie's mother controlled the five women from the village who helped there with the ruthless efficiency of a Harvard MBA graduate. Talk about the iron fist in the oven glove.

'How is Bram getting on, anyway?' her mother asked as she went back to rolling pastry. When Sophie tried to make pastry she got flour everywhere, but Harriet's apron was pristine. 'It must be difficult for him now Molly's gone.'

Sophie clambered awkwardly onto one of the modern stools at the breakfast bar. 'He's managing.'

'He needs to find himself a wife.' Intent on her pastry, Harriet didn't notice Sophie's instinctive start. What was this? A conspiracy? 'I heard that Rachel took herself off to York,' she went on, before Sophie had a chance to reply. 'I didn't think she'd last long.'

'Mum, you hardly knew her!'

'You didn't need to know her. You just needed to look at her.' Harriet clicked her tongue against her teeth. 'I could have told Bram that he was wasting his time a long time ago. A city girl like that is no good to him. He needs someone who can help him make a go of that farm. There's good land up there. He could do so much more with it.'

Harriet was a great believer in diversification. 'You can't get by on farming alone nowadays,' she would tell anyone who would listen. 'You've got to try something different.' She herself had an excellent business brain, and Sophie had often suspected that she had been bored as a farmer's wife until yet another agricultural crisis had prompted her to set up her own catering company.

It had been such a success that Harriet was always encouraging farmers like Bram to follow her example

and branch out. She thought he should convert his stead-
ings into holiday cottages, offer shooting weekends, or
turn his lower fields into a par three golf course. She
seemed frustrated that Bram was apparently content to
stick with farming sheep and cattle at Haw Gill, as generations of Thoresbys had done before him.

'I'm very fond of Bram,' Harriet often said, tutting,
'but he's got no ambition. He's not going anywhere.'

But it seemed to Sophie that Bram was already exactly
where he wanted to be. He had no need to go anywhere
at all.

'It's just as well Melissa didn't marry Bram,' Harriet
said now. 'He wouldn't have been able to offer her the
kind of life she's used to. Look at Haw Gill. That farmhouse has hardly changed in fifty years!'

No, and as a result it was so much more comfortable
than Glebe Farm, Sophie thought to herself.

'Anyway, she's much better off with Nick,' her
mother said with satisfaction. 'His company's doing very
well, you know. He can look after her.'

Spoil her, you mean, Sophie corrected her mother, but
only mentally. She wouldn't waste her breath saying it
out loud.

'Melissa and Bram were far too young to get engaged.' Harriet continued her train of thought. 'Your father said so at the time, and he was right. It would never
have worked. But it was a shame for Bram. I do wonder
sometimes if he's still got a soft spot for Melissa. He
never seems to have got close to settling down with anyone else. It does seem a waste. He's a nice young man.'

Bram was more than *nice*, thought Sophie, vaguely
aggrieved but not quite sure why. It wasn't as if she
hadn't always known that Bram was in love with
Melissa.

'Did he tell you about Vicky Manning?' her mother was asking, laying the circle of pastry over a pie dish. She cut off the excess with a few swift, clean movements and began knocking up the edges with the back of the knife.

'No.' Sophie was surprised at the apparent *non sequitur*. Vicky had been in the year below her at school. She was a plump, pretty girl, nice enough, but a bit wishy-washy in Sophie's opinion. 'What about her?'

'She was supposed to be getting married in less than a month,' Harriet told her. 'They'd booked that hotel over Whitby way. Her dress was made and the invitations had gone out and everything, and then her fiancé Keith lost his nerve and called the whole thing off! He's gone off to Manchester to get a job, and Vicky's been left to pick up all the pieces. She devastated, apparently.'

'Oh, poor thing!' Vicky might not be the most interesting person in the world, but no one deserved to be treated like that. Sophie knew how Vicky must feel. She might not have got as far as sending out invitations or choosing a dress herself, but that didn't make the rejection and humiliation any easier to bear. 'I'm really sorry,' she said sincerely.

'It's hard on her,' Harriet agreed, 'but I dare say it's all for the best. According to Maggie, Keith was always going on about how boring it was up here, and hankering after the bright lights, but Vicky wouldn't have wanted to move. She's a real country girl.'

She checked the temperature on the oven, put in the pie and closed the door, wiping her hands on a teatowel. 'I wouldn't be surprised if she ended up with Bram,' she said.

'Bram?' Sophie sat up straight on her stool, outraged. 'Vicky's not the right girl for Bram!'

'Well, I don't know...' Harriet considered the matter as she wiped down the work surface. 'She could do with losing a bit of weight, but she's got a sweet little face and she's a hard worker. She's grown up on the moors, too. I think she would make a good farmer's wife.'

'Maybe, but not Bram's,' said Sophie stubbornly.

'Beggars can't be choosers,' said Harriet. 'There aren't that many suitable girls around here. Bram will need to settle down soon, if he wants to have children. He's certainly not getting any younger.'

And neither are you. Sophie didn't know why her mother didn't say it out loud.

'Bram's only thirty-two, Mother. He's not exactly decrepit!'

'He'll need to be getting on with it,' said Harriet firmly. 'I don't know why you're all so picky nowadays. If you wait too long for someone perfect, you'll have lost your chance. Look at you and that Rob,' she went on in an aggrieved tone. 'He sounded so nice, and all you can say is that it didn't feel right.'

Sophie sighed. She didn't want to start this argument again. 'It *didn't* feel right, Mum. You can't marry someone just because they're available and you're not sure if you'll find anyone better! And now I've met someone else. I told you that.'

Her mind flashed to Bram, and she thought about what he'd said. What would it be like to be able to say, *Look, it's Bram, Mum. We're in love and we're going to get married!* What would her mother say? Would she believe it?

Not that she could say that now. They had decided it was impossible.

As it was. Quite impossible.

So impossible she really had to stop thinking about it.

Her mother was not to be convinced. 'And how do you know this *secret someone* is going to be any better than Rob?' she demanded, checking the pots that were boiling on the stove and banging down the lids with unnecessary force.

'He might be.'

'Well, if he can't even bring himself to reveal his name, I don't suppose he'll be committing himself to Christmas,' said Harriet, and something in her voice told Sophie that a dose of emotional blackmail was coming up.

She sighed inwardly. 'We haven't talked about Christmas yet.'

'Because if he can't make it—and I'm sure he'll have his own family to go to—I thought I might ask Bram to Christmas lunch. He's practically family anyway, and I don't like the idea of him being on his own at Christmas.'

This was a change of tack. Sophie looked at her mother suspiciously, unsure what was coming next. 'I thought you'd have him married off to Vicky Manning by Christmas?'

'Don't be silly, dear. It would be much too soon for that. No, this will be Bram's first Christmas without Molly, and I think we should look after him. I'm sure he'd like to see you. You're such good friends, after all.'

She paused. 'Of course it wouldn't be much fun for him if you weren't here,' she continued airily. 'Nick and Melissa can be a bit lovey-dovey sometimes, and he wouldn't want to feel a gooseberry—especially if he *is* still hankering after Melissa.'

Ah, there it was! Sophie had no trouble interpreting the subtext to this one. By refusing to come home for Christmas Sophie would not only be heartlessly denying

her potentially frail father the pleasure of a last
Christmas in the family home, but she would also be
condemning Bram to a solitary Yuletide celebration with
only his grief for company.

Her 'frail' father had spent the day bringing sheep
down off the moor, and at breakfast he had looked in
rude health, but Sophie had already made the decision
to come home to celebrate his birthday. Which meant
staying for Christmas, too.

But she might not dread it quite so much if she had
Bram there for moral support. Why not let her mother
think that she had successfully blackmailed her into
Christmas at last?

'That sounds a great idea, Mum,' she said. 'Of course
I'll come.'

Sophie turned up her collar against the November drizzle
and left the shelter of the tube station to walk back to
her flat, feeling depressed. She was now officially without a job—and, more to the point, without an income.
The rent was due at the end of the month and she had
no idea how she was going to pay it.

She couldn't say that the redundancy was unexpected.
They had all known that the axe was going to fall sooner
or later, and the atmosphere in the office had been tense,
to say the least, for some time now. Sophie wasn't the
first person to lose their job, and she wouldn't be the
last.

It wasn't as if it had broken her heart to leave either.
Selling insurance for computing systems had to be the
dullest of jobs. Maybe some of her colleagues found it
fascinating, Sophie acknowledged fairly, but with her
dreams of making it as a successful potter it had been
dreary work.

Still, she had been lucky to find a job at all. She had left art college with such high hopes, but had soon discovered that it was tough to make a living as a potter in London. It hadn't been long before she had settled for an office job to pay the rent while she worked on her pottery in the evenings and at weekends. Finding a gallery to show her work earlier that year had been her first step towards her longed-for career, but even that had folded now.

Sophie sighed. London was so expensive, too. It would be easier if she could go home to the moors—but even there jobs weren't that easy to come by. And, she would never be able to earn enough for her own house, which meant that she would have to live at home, and she and her mother could barely manage a weekend without clashing.

No, living with her parents was not an option—and anyway, it wouldn't change the real reason she hesitated about going home.

Nick.

She would be bound to bump into him all the time. At her parents'. In the supermarket. In the pub. The anguish of seeing him but not being able to touch him would be too much to bear.

So London it had to be. Except that she hated it here. All week it had been grey and miserable. The traffic seemed to be permanently jammed, exhaust fumes mingling in the grimy air with the sound of engines and blaring horns and distant sirens. There always seemed to be an alarm going off somewhere, ringing frantically while everyone else ignored it completely.

And all week Sophie had been gripped by a terrible homesickness. It was always there, like a low, persistent ache, but this week it had sharpened to a longing so acute she sometimes felt physically sick.

That was Bram's fault. He had dangled the possibility of going home before her eyes, and now she couldn't stop thinking about it. She tidied up the remains of a takeaway in the flat's cramped kitchen and thought about Haw Gill. The kitchen window in the flat had a view across grim yards to the back of an identical terrace; at Haw Gill you looked out onto a sweep of moor and a big Yorkshire sky.

She could be there. The thought niggled at Sophie. The kitchen at Haw Gill could be hers.

If she married Bram.

It had been the right decision to say no, Sophie told herself endlessly. To marry him without love would be using him, and she couldn't do that to Bram.

But what if he was right? What if he never met that special woman she had wished for him? What if he decided to settle for second best after all, since he couldn't have Melissa? What if he looked at someone like Vicky Manning and decided that she would do?

That was the thought that really rankled with Sophie. She kept remembering what her mother had said about Vicky making a good farmer's wife. Vicky wouldn't complain about life on the moors, but Bram would be bored to death in a year, Sophie was sure. He would be too loyal to do anything about it, though, and then he'd be stuck with Vicky for life.

At least she could save him from that fate. She might not be his perfect woman, but she would be a better wife for him than Vicky.

And she could go home.

And she would be able to face Nick and Melissa.

It all made sense…didn't it?

Her flatmate, Ella, was all for it. 'Why on earth did you say no?' she had demanded when Sophie had told her about Bram's proposition. 'It seems to me that marrying this Bram would solve all your problems. You could go back to your moors, you wouldn't have to find another job, it would get your mother off your back, and, most importantly, it would be one in the eye for that slimeball who dumped you for your sister!'

'He's not a slimeball,' Sophie had protested, as she always did, but Ella refused to listen to a good word about Nick.

'He didn't do right by you,' she would insist to Sophie. 'If he'd fallen in love with Melissa he shouldn't have made it obvious until he'd had a chance to talk to you. Instead, he let you do all his dirty work. Nick goes on and on about what a great guy he is, but if you ask me, he's not a gentleman!'

Which always sounded odd coming from someone with a nose stud and pierced eyebrows.

'I couldn't marry Bram,' Sophie tried to explain later that Friday night, as they sat over a bottle of wine, both of them unable to afford to go out. 'He's my oldest friend.'

'So? There's nothing in the rule book that says you can't marry an old friend. Friendship ought to be a plus. Is there something wrong with him?'

'Of course not!'

'No spitty lips? No hairy nostrils?'

Sophie couldn't help laughing. 'No!'

'So what does he look like?' asked Ella, leaning precariously from the armchair where she was sprawled to fill up Sophie's glass on the floor.

'Bram? He's nothing special.' Just for a moment Sophie thought of Bram's blue eyes, of the warmth of his slow smile, of his air of solid strength. 'But he's not ugly either. He's just…Bram.'

'Hmm.' Ella wriggled back into a comfortable position and eyed Sophie over her glass. 'And have the two of you ever…you know?'

'No!' Sophie squirmed uncomfortably at the thought.

'Not even a kiss?'

'No.'

'I can't believe you never even thought about it,' said Ella sceptically. 'I mean, the two of you up there on the moors…he's a man, you're a woman…you're both single…neither of you are grotesque…you *must* have imagined what it would be like!'

'No, we haven't,' said Sophie firmly. 'Bram and I really *are* just good friends. There's never been any question of…you know, anything physical. Anyway, he's in love with Melissa.'

'Not that much in love with her if he's offered to marry you,' Ella pointed out.

'He's only done that because he knows I'm not in love with him and I understand how he feels about Melissa.'

'Well, if you don't want him, and he needs consoling, maybe he'd like to marry me,' sighed Ella. 'I wouldn't mind a hunky farmer.'

Sophie knew her friend was joking, but a little part of her bristled at the very idea of Ella and Bram together. That really would be all wrong.

'I don't think you'd like being a farmer's wife,' she said, as lightly as she could. 'You have to get up very early. Anyway, what about Steve? I thought you wanted to marry him?'

Ella's face darkened. 'Don't mention his name to me! He thinks he can come and go as he pleases. And if that's Mr Lack-of-Commitment now,' she added as the phone began to ring, 'tell him I'm out!'

'Are you sure?' Sophie looked doubtful. Ella had been keen on Steve for a very long time.

'Yes. I'm not going to come running whenever he whistles any more. Let him learn what it feels like for a change!'

'OK.' Obediently, Sophie leant down from the sofa and reached for the cordless phone—which had been left on the floor as usual. It was just too far away to get at easily, and she had to practically roll off the sofa to scrabble at it with her fingers, but at last it was within her grasp.

'Hello?'

'Sophie, it's Melissa.'

'Mel!' Sophie's heart sank. She loved her sister dearly, but conversations with her now were often difficult. Melissa had a tendency to get tearful, and was so bound up in guilt about what she called 'stealing' Nick from Sophie that Sophie was usually exhausted from the effort of making her feel better by the time she put down the phone. She simply didn't have the energy to be bouncy and positive tonight, but if she wasn't Melissa would accuse her of being depressed because of Nick and feel even worse.

'How are you?' she asked, fixing on a bright smile to make her voice sound better.

'I'm fine.'

'And Nick?' she made herself ask.

'He's great,' said Melissa, although Sophie thought she sounded faintly on edge. 'He's away this weekend, climbing in Scotland. He's leading a group,' she explained. 'Well, he's not the official leader, but they like him to go along because he's so experienced.'

OK, thought Sophie. She could practically hear Nick saying that, but it didn't explain the tension in her sister's voice. Surely she didn't suspect Nick of using the climbing trip as a cover for meeting another woman? How could Nick even think of looking at anyone else when he had Melissa?

'He sends his love,' said Melissa dutifully.

Did he, now? Sophie couldn't prevent the clench of her heart at the thought of Nick's love. She could quite imagine him gaily telling Melissa to send his love to her sister, without even thinking how she would feel to hear his love passed on at second hand.

'So,' she said brightly, 'what's new?'

'Oh, nothing, really,' said Melissa with a faint sigh. 'I was just ringing about Dad's birthday. Mum's so thrilled that you're coming after all. She was afraid you'd make another excuse, and I didn't want to have to tell them why you feel uncomfortable about being at Glebe Farm when Nick and I are there.

'I think it's wonderful of you to come,' Melissa went on. 'It'll mean so much to Dad, too. I just…just hope it's not going to be too difficult for you.'

'I'll be fine,' said Sophie, trying to ward off the inevitable guilty spiel.

'You always *say* that,' said Melissa desperately, 'but I know you're just being brave. Nick knows too. He really understands how hard it'll be for you to meet him again. He knows how much you loved him, and I do too, of course…

'Oh, Sophie,' she said, her voice breaking. 'I so wish things could have been different! You're such a wonderful person, and you deserve to be happy. I can't bear the thought of you on your own.'

'Melissa, I'm *fine*,' said Sophie wearily. 'Really I am.

I've moved on. Honestly, I hardly think about Nick any more.'

A lie, of course, but Melissa wasn't to know that.

'But you're still on your own. We'll be sitting on one side of the table at Christmas lunch and you'll be on the other, and it's just going to be *awful* for you, I know it,' said Melissa, on the verge of tears.

Sophie set her jaw. 'I won't be on my own, Mel. Bram will be there.'

'It's not the same,' she said stubbornly. 'I don't mean it won't be lovely to have him there,' Melissa added, as if afraid that she had been rude. 'He's so nice, and such a good friend, and he must be missing Molly a lot. Is it true that he's seeing Vicky Manning now? Did he tell you?'

'What?' Sophie sat up straight.

'Nick said that he saw them in the pub together the other night. I suppose you heard about her wedding being called off?'

'Yes, Mum told me,' said Sophie slowly. *She* was usually the only person who went to the pub with Bram. What was he doing there with Vicky?

'It must be awful for her, poor thing,' Melissa said. 'And so humiliating. I think she's being really brave about it. Apparently she's telling everyone that she just has to accept what's happened and get on with her life. I'm not sure I'd have been able to do that if *my* fiancé had dumped me just before—'

She broke off, realising too late what she had said. 'Oh, Sophie, I'm sorry,' she wailed. 'I didn't think…'

'It's all right, Melissa, honestly.' Sophie would say anything to stop her sister dissolving into tears again. 'Tell Vicky to look at me.'

And tell her to leave Bram alone, she added mentally.

'At you?'

'I'm living proof that life goes on and that you can be happy again,' said Sophie, injecting as much happiness as she could into her voice. 'And so is Bram. Remember how upset he was when you broke off your engagement? But look at him now. He's fine.'

Even if he hadn't ever got over Melissa properly. That was something else she wouldn't tell Melissa.

'I suppose so.' Melissa didn't sound convinced, so perhaps she knew Bram better than Sophie thought she did. Well, she had been engaged to him, hadn't she?

'I wish he could find someone else,' she went on with a sigh. Bram was another person Melissa spent a lot of time feeling guilty about. 'I hope it works out with Vicky. Nick said he certainly looked as if he was keen.'

Oh, did he? Sophie thought furiously. Bram had no business looking keen on Vicky barely a few days after he'd been suggesting marriage to *her*!

'Of course it's probably still a bit soon for Vicky,' Melissa was rambling on, unaware of Sophie's mental interjection. 'But I think they'd be good together, don't you?'

'Bram and Vicky?' said Sophie incredulously. 'No, I don't!'

She could practically see Melissa's perfect brow wrinkling in a puzzled expression. 'But why not? They're both so sweet-natured. Vicky would be perfect for Bram. She really knows what life is like on a hill farm, and she loves the moors. And Bram does need a wife,' she reminded Sophie.

'He may do,' said Sophie, goaded, 'but he's not marrying Vicky. He's marrying me!'

CHAPTER FOUR

'YOU'VE done it now,' said Ella, when Sophie finally managed to get Melissa off the phone.

'I don't care,' said Sophie stoutly, although actually she was beginning to feel a bit sick about what she had done. She told Ella what Melissa had said. 'I couldn't let her foist Vicky Manning on Bram like that!'

'Aha, I thought that Vicky might be at the root of all this! You're jealous of her.'

'I am *not*,' insisted Sophie. She tossed her head. 'If you must know, I feel very sorry for her. It's bad enough being dumped by your fiancé without everyone in the village rushing to set you up with the only available man. I mean, they were only having a drink in the pub. Bram's the kind of guy who does buy you a drink if you're lonely. He's kind that way. It doesn't mean he's interested in her or that he's going to *marry* her!'

'But you wouldn't like it if he did,' said Ella shrewdly.

'Only because she's all wrong for him.'

Ella looked innocently at the ceiling. 'The words *dog* and *manger* spring to mind,' she said.

'Look, Bram's my best friend. I know what he needs, and it isn't Vicky Manning!'

'It isn't you, either,' Ella pointed out.

Sophie shifted uncomfortably. 'I shouldn't have said that we were getting married, should I?' she admitted. 'I wasn't really thinking. It was just that Melissa was going on and on about how Bram was still on his own, and it was as if the whole village has already decided that he and Vicky might as well get together and tie up a couple of awkward loose ends.

'Bram deserves better than that,' she said, on the defensive now. 'I suppose I got cross, and the words were out before I knew what I was going to say.' She bit her lip. 'I didn't mean it.'

'You'd better ring Melissa back, then, and tell her that.'

'I *can't*. She was so thrilled when I told her. She said that now we could all be happy, that Bram and I were perfect for each other, and on and on... I thought she was never going to stop telling me what wonderful news it was!'

Sophie grimaced, remembering her sister's ecstasies. 'If I tell her that I lied, she'll want to know why, and what could I tell her? Whatever I say, she'll just think it means that I was trying to compensate for losing Nick, and then she'll get upset because that'll convince her that I'm still not over him and it's all her fault, and, really, I can't go through all that again tonight!'

'She's probably already on the phone to Mum, and Mum will tell Maggie Jackson, and once Maggie knows we might as well take out a full-page advertisement in the *Askerby and District Gazette*!'

Sophie put her head in her hands. 'Oh, God, what have I done?'

'Just got yourself engaged to your best friend without telling him,' said Ella, who seemed to be enjoying Sophie's predicament far more than a real friend ought to.

'What shall I do?' Sophie asked her, too appalled now at what she had done even to resent Ella's good humour.

'Well, if you can't face Melissa again, it sounds as if

you'd better let Bram know what's going on before the *Askerby Gazette* gets hold of it.'

'Yes, of course.' Sophie jerked up, propelling herself into action. 'I'll call him right now.'

She checked her watch. Just after ten. Farmers were notorious for going to bed early, and Bram was no exception, but she might still get him.

Reaching for the phone, she began stabbing at the numbers, but was in such a state that she got the code all wrong and had to start again.

'What are you going to say to him?' asked Ella. 'You can't just tell him that he's marrying you!'

'We don't actually have to go through with it, do we?' Sophie fortified herself with a gulp of wine and forced herself to dial more slowly. She was beginning to think more clearly. 'We can just pretend we are until all the fuss dies down and then say that we've changed our minds. All Bram has to do is play along for a while. He'll do that for me,' she said, wishing that she felt as confident as she sounded.

She could imagine the phone ringing in the kitchen at Haw Gill. It usually sat on the dresser. If Bram was up, he should be able to get to it within two or three rings. But the phone rang on and on.

'*Please* don't have gone to bed, Bram,' Sophie muttered. What was she going to do if she got the answer machine? It wasn't the kind of thing you could leave as a message. *Oh, by the way, I've told Melissa we're getting married. Hope that's OK. See you soon. Bye!*

'Haw Gill Farm.'

The sound of that deep, slow, steady voice left Sophie light-headed with relief.

'Oh, thank God you're there!' she rushed in without preliminaries. 'I've got to talk to you!'

'*Sophie?*'

He sounded a little odd. 'I didn't wake you up, did I?' she asked.

'No…no.' There was a distinct note of hesitation in his voice, though. 'This isn't a very good time,' he added carefully.

'What do you mean?'

Another slightly awkward pause. 'Well…Vicky's here.'

'*Vicky?*'

'Vicky Manning. You remember her, don't you?'

Sophie held the phone away from her and stared at it very hard for a moment.

'Yes, I remember her,' she said tightly, bringing the phone back to her ear. 'What's she doing there?'

She'd meant the question to come out light and amused, but had a horrible feeling that instead she had sounded hostile and—worse—jealous.

'Waiting for me to make her a cup of coffee,' said Bram.

Coffee. Right. Sophie's heart sank.

She had been able—more or less—to dismiss Nick's account of seeing him with Vicky in the pub. After all, there was no reason why he shouldn't meet up and have a drink with her there.

But if he had taken Vicky home, that meant something else. Asking someone in for coffee in London didn't mean much, but Haw Gill Farm was so isolated that you didn't just casually suggest dropping in on the way home.

Which meant that Bram probably had more in mind than small talk over a mug of instant.

A sick feeling churned in the pit of Sophie's stomach. It wasn't that she was jealous—not really—but Bram and *Vicky*? Vicky was all wrong for him. Surely Bram could see that?

'Is it important?' Bram asked in that same cautious tone when she didn't say anything.

'Of course it's important or I wouldn't be ringing you at this hour!' snapped Sophie, ruffled more than she wanted to admit by the knowledge that Vicky was there...with Bram.

God, what if it *were* serious? What if Bram and Vicky were the new couple in the district? Melissa would get wind of it in no time, and then what would Sophie be able to say? *Oh, I was just joking when I told you I was marrying Bram?*

Cue more tearful guilt for Melissa and more humiliation for Sophie.

She lowered her voice. 'Can Vicky hear you?'

'No, she's in the sitting room.' Instinctively, Bram dropped his voice to match hers.

The sitting room at Haw Gill Farm was traditionally reserved for special occasions. Sophie didn't know whether that was a good sign or a bad one. If Bram were really comfortable with Vicky, they would just be sitting around the kitchen table.

On the other hand, there was something very inviting about the sitting room on a winter night, when the red curtains were drawn against the weather. Sophie could picture Vicky curled up winsomely on the hearthrug in front of the fire. There would be no lamps on, just the flickering light of the flames. She would be waiting for Bram to come back with the coffee.

Who was that? she would say when he came in, smiling up at him with her big blue eyes and that little gap between her teeth that was supposed to be so sexy.

And Bram would put the mugs down on the hearth

and pull her down as he stretched on the rug beside her. *Nobody important,* he would say.

That little scenario didn't make Sophie feel any better at all.

'Look, Bram, is it serious between you and Vicky? I mean, do you really like her?'

Sophie was beginning to think that she had made a terrible mistake. If there was something between Bram and Vicky then she had quite possibly ruined it by telling Melissa a stupid lie.

'Sophie, we are just having a cup of coffee together— or were until you interrupted us. What is it that is so important?'

'Well,' she said nervously. 'I just thought that I should warn you that I've sort of told Melissa that we're getting married.'

Silence. Not just silence. *Deafening* silence. It seemed to resonate down the phone. Sophie would almost rather he had shouted.

'I'm sorry, I know I shouldn't have done it,' she rushed on. 'But Melissa rang and she was talking about you and Vicky and somehow it just…slipped out.'

'Slipped out?' Bram found his voice at last. 'How can something like that *just slip out*?'

'Look, it was your idea,' Sophie pointed out defensively.

'*My* idea?'

'You were the one who suggested that we should get married.'

'Oh, that idea,' said Bram. 'Would that be the one that you refused to consider the other day?'

Sophie scowled. She didn't like it when Bram was sarcastic. 'I *did* consider it,' she protested. 'I just didn't think that it would be a good idea.'

'But now you do?'

'Yes… No…' Sophie found herself floundering. He was supposed to be sympathising and making her smile, the way he always did. He was supposed to make everything better, the way he always did. He *wasn't* supposed to be making her feel a complete and utter fool, the way he was doing.

'We wouldn't need to actually get married,' she tried to explain. 'I thought we could just pretend for a couple of weeks. Then we could tell everyone that we've changed our minds.'

Bram glanced at the kitchen door, hoping that Vicky wouldn't start wondering what had happened to him. 'If we're not going to get married, what's the point of pretending that we are?'

'To stop Melissa thinking I'm nuts! What do you think?' Sophie was getting cross. She really wanted to go off and be quiet somewhere so she could work out how she had got into this situation.

She took a breath and made herself speak more calmly. 'Look, I'm sorry. I know I've dumped this on you without warning, but we're not talking about a lifetime's commitment here. I'm only asking you to cover me for a few weeks, and after that you can invite Vicky back as much as you want. But until then could you *please* play along?' she added desperately. 'Especially when Mum rings you.'

'Your mother's going to ring *me*?' For the first time Bram sounded alarmed—as well he might. Harriet Beckwith's powers of interrogation were legendary.

'Well, she might do,' said Sophie. 'Melissa is bound to tell her first thing tomorrow, if she hasn't already, and it wouldn't surprise me if she tried to get hold of us.

She'll probably ring me first, but I don't want to talk to her until we've got our story straight.'

Bram sighed. 'What exactly did you tell Melissa?' he asked, making a mental vow not to answer the phone at all the following day.

They were both still whispering, which seemed absurd. Sophie cleared her throat and made an effort to talk more normally.

'I just said that we'd fallen in love and decided to get married.'

'And she believed you?'

'Funnily enough, she did,' said Sophie, suddenly awkward. 'She seemed to think that we were made for each other. I don't know why. I gave her all that stuff you told me, about suddenly looking at someone and seeing them in a completely different light, so maybe that convinced her. Only I thought it might be stretching coincidence a bit if it happened to us both at the same time, so I said you'd realised earlier but hadn't wanted to say anything because you thought I just wanted to be friends. I hope that's OK?' she finished nervously.

'So Melissa now thinks I didn't have the guts to tell you I was in love with you until you gave me the right opening?'

'Melissa knows you're not like that,' said Sophie impatiently. 'As far as she's concerned you're sensitive and patient, and you loved me too much to jeopardise our friendship, but when I was up last weekend I just looked at you and the scales fell from my eyes. I realised that it was you I had loved all along, so of course then we…you know, fell into each other's arms…and that was that.'

'I see,' said Bram. 'Melissa bought that?'

'She seemed to.'

Melissa had done more than buy it. She had marvelled at her own stupidity in not being able to see it for herself.

'You're perfect together,' she had cried. 'Oh, this is wonderful news! Bram's such a lovely person, and so are you. It's so obvious that you belong together! I can't believe none of us ever saw it coming. I suppose you've always been such good friends that it never occurred to us to think of you as anything else,' she'd decided in the end.

'If you told her all that, it doesn't sound as if there's much chance of convincing her that we've decided it was all just a silly mistake in a couple of weeks,' said Bram wryly. 'Which means that as far as everyone here is concerned we're now engaged.'

'I'm afraid so,' said Sophie in a small voice. 'But I won't make you stick to it, I promise, Bram. I'll behave really badly, if you want, so no one will blame you for breaking our engagement off when the time comes.'

'We'd better not break it off just yet or Melissa really will get suspicious,' he said. He glanced towards the door again. 'Look, I'd better go, or Vicky will wonder whether I'm growing the coffee beans out here.'

Sophie had forgotten Vicky for a minute. 'What will you tell her?'

'I'm not sure yet.'

'Oh.' That sounded suspiciously as if he was hoping to keep his options open. Surely he wouldn't tell Vicky the truth, would he? Sophie didn't have the nerve to ask, though. Bram had put up with a lot already.

'If we're going to be in love, I need you here to back me up,' Bram was saying. 'I'm not pretending all by myself. How soon can you get up here?'

'I'm not exactly overwhelmed with commitments

down here,' said Sophie, thinking of her non-existent job. 'What about tomorrow?'

'Let me know when your train gets in. I'll pick you up from the station. And then,' said Bram, with just a touch of grimness in his voice, 'I think we'd better talk.'

The mud-spattered Land Rover was waiting just outside the station entrance when Sophie arrived the following afternoon. It was only half past three, but the meagre light of a dull, wet November day was already rapidly fading and the street lamps were blurred and yellow in the creeping mist.

Bram leant across Bess, who was sitting next to him on the front seat, to open the passenger door for her. 'Hi,' said Sophie as she climbed in, the way she had hundreds of times before. She wanted to be casual and friendly, the way she always was with Bram, but instead her voice sounded high and brittle, as if she were nervous.

She *was* nervous. Sophie had never been nervous around Bram before, and it felt *horrible*, but the more she thought about the enormity of what she had done, the more nervous she felt. She had told a stupid lie to her sister which meant that she had interrupted his evening, put him in an awkward position with Vicky, and without asking she had committed him to a ridiculous pretence that soon everyone in the village would know about.

She had taken him for granted, the way she always did, but this time she had gone too far. She had heard it in his voice last night, a certain reserve, just a hint of sternness and exasperation that was so unlike Bram's usual dry humour that it had made Sophie realise how much she depended on his approval. She felt as if she had forfeited that with her rash announcement to Melissa, and she didn't like it at all.

'Good journey?' he asked.

'Not too bad. We were a bit late leaving King's Cross, but at least we weren't delayed by ''leaves on the line''.'

Oh, God, they were making small talk. This was *awful*.

As Bram checked his mirror and pulled away, Sophie put on her seat belt and made a big thing of patting Bess, who was panting happily between them, content just to be close to her master.

Why couldn't her life be like Bess's? A dog's needs were so simple. All Bess wanted was to be fed and to be near Bram at all times. Heaven would be to be allowed into the kitchen to sit at his feet by the fire. Even a dog had to have a dream.

Sophie wished that it could be that easy for her. Bess had Bram to look after her all the time, and she never got into a muddle or did stupid things that made Bram cross.

Well, sometimes she did, Sophie amended to herself. She had once seen Bess get thoroughly muddled by Bram's whistled instructions and the sheep had bolted in the wrong direction, which hadn't gone down very well. But he was never angry for long, and Bess was so adoring and put her ears down so placatingly that he never carried out his threat to send her back and get a proper dog.

The silence lengthened uncomfortably. 'Thanks for coming to pick me up,' Sophie tried, falling back on small talk once more.

'We're engaged, aren't we? Picking girlfriends up at the station is the kind of thing fiancés do.' Bram sounded quite terse. He joined the queue of cars waiting to turn out of the station, drumming his fingers on the wheel as they inched forward.

Maybe she could try flattening her own ears, thought Sophie. It worked for Bess.

'I'm sorry about all this, Bram,' she said awkwardly. 'I've been feeling really bad about forcing an engagement on you. I should have thought before I opened my big mouth.'

'Well, it's done now,' he said, putting on his indicator to turn right. 'We're going to have to make the best of it now. Three people have congratulated me already today—and that's not counting the postman, who wanted to know when the wedding was to be.'

Oh, God. It was real, then. And all her fault.

Sophie swallowed. Mindlessly fondling Bess's silky ears, she studied Bram from under her lashes. In the darkness of the car he suddenly seemed like a stranger, his face lit only by the fuzzy orange glow of the station lights. For the first time she saw him not as Bram, not as the boy she remembered so well, but as a man. There was a solidity and a strength to him as he sat there, power in the big hands on the wheel, toughness in the set of his jaw.

This was the man she had so casually claimed that she was going to marry. The man everybody in Askerby now thought was in love with her. They might imagine him kissing her with that stern mouth, undressing her with those sure hands, making love to her in the farmhouse up on the moor. A strange feeling that was not quite a shiver shuddered down Sophie's spine and she jerked her gaze away from him.

Not a very helpful way to be thinking. She had caused Bram enough trouble, without confusing the situation even further by starting to think of him…like that. If they were going to get through this she needed to keep a cool head.

'I hope I didn't spoil your evening completely last night,' she said.

'Let's just say that it didn't turn out quite the way that I expected,' said Bram, as a car flashed its headlights and let him pull out into the other lane. There was an undercurrent of irony in his voice that made Sophie look at him sharply.

That was the wrong reply. And definitely the wrong tone of voice. *It was no big deal,* would have been an acceptable answer. Or, even better, *To be honest, I was glad of the interruption. I realised I'd made a mistake as soon as we left the pub.* Nothing that implied he had hoped the evening would end very differently, anyway.

Bess sighed and settled down, resting her head in Sophie's lap. 'How long have you and Vicky been seeing each other?' Sophie stroked her soft ears. 'You didn't say anything about it last weekend.'

'That's because there wasn't anything to say. We had a drink in the pub, went back for coffee, and then you rang. So we drank the coffee and I took her home. I don't call that "seeing each other".'

That was a better answer. Sophie cheered up a bit.

'I wouldn't have said that Vicky was your type, anyway,' she said.

'Why not?'

'Well…I don't know,' she said, a little thrown by the abruptness of his question. 'I guess she's not like your other girlfriends. Rachel, for instance.'

Vicky was nothing like Melissa either, but Sophie didn't think it would be tactful to mention that.

'Girls like Rachel aren't interested in spending their lives in the middle of the Yorkshire moors,' said Bram, without taking his eyes from the road. 'Maybe it's time I changed my type. At least Vicky is at home on a farm. She's a nice person, too. She's had a bad time, being dumped by her fiancé. She knows what it's like to have to let go of things. She's quiet and sensible and pretty... I could do a lot worse.'

Sophie stared at him, appalled. He couldn't be serious, could he? 'Well, I'm sorry if I interrupted the beginning of a beautiful friendship,' she said snippily, forgetting her resolve to stay cool and in control. 'You should have told me to forget it when I rang!'

'How could I?' said Bram. 'News of our engagement is already all over Askerby. It's a good thing you rang when you did, otherwise Vicky might have thought that I'd been messing her around.'

In other words, if she hadn't rung the two of them would have been doing more than seeing each other! Sophie's throat was tight with confusion and misery and guilt—and relief that she had called when she had. It would have been too late otherwise.

'As it is, the gossips are going to have a field-day,' Bram went on. 'Last night they all saw Vicky and I leave the pub together, and this morning they hear I'm engaged to you. I just hope none of it upsets Vicky. She's had enough to deal with recently.'

'How was I to know that you'd be inviting stray women back for coffee?' demanded Sophie, hurt and angry, but unable to justify feeling either. 'It was only last weekend that you were suggesting that *I* marry you. You can't blame me for not realising that you would go straight out and try to find someone else!'

'It wasn't like that,' said Bram. The traffic lights changed to red and he stopped, jerking on the handbrake with a little extra vehemence.

'Oh? Then how *was* it?'

He stared ahead, resting his hands on the top of the steering wheel. 'I suppose it was just that after you turned down my idea of getting married I realised that it really was time to face up to things,' he said slowly. 'If I really wanted to find a wife and have a family I would have to forget about Melissa and move on. So I decided to go out to the pub. Not a very dramatic change of life, but I don't usually go during the week.

'It just happened that Vicky was there. She was obviously lonely, and we got talking. And she was there the next time I went down, too. I'm not pretending I fell madly in love, but I thought, Why waste any more time? If I was going to find a new relationship I had to start somewhere, and we had to get beyond just chatting in the pub.

'So I asked if she wanted to come and have coffee at Haw Gill, but she couldn't talk about anything except Keith. She's pretty raw about the way he cancelled the wedding. I felt sorry for her,' said Bram as the lights changed and he released the brake once more. 'She doesn't deserve to be hurt like that.'

Sophie didn't say anything. She should have been nicer about Vicky, she thought guiltily, mindlessly stroking Bess. If anyone ought to understand how the other girl was feeling right now, it was her. She knew what it was like to discover that all your dreams were not going to come true after all. But she had been bitchy, not kind. Jealous instead of sympathetic.

She was a cow. No wonder Bram was fed up. Who would want everyone thinking that he was desperate enough to consider being lumbered with her for life? It wasn't surprising that they were all pushing him towards Vicky Manning.

Beside her, Bram glanced at her averted profile and felt awful. He had spoken without thinking. Sophie didn't need to be told what Vicky was going through. She hadn't deserved to be hurt either. Now all he had done was remind her of Nick.

Nice one, Bram.

He had been unprepared for the sharpness of the disappointment he had felt when Sophie had turned down the idea of marriage the previous weekend. The more Bram had thought about it, the more he'd thought it would work. They could have a good marriage. He and Sophie were such good friends—surely that would make up for the fact that they weren't passionately in love?

Bram had been well on his way to convincing himself that he really did want to marry Sophie, and it had been harder than he'd thought when she had said no.

But he was determined not to waste any more of his life. Sophie had said no, and that was that. Until then he had only talked about moving on, but trying to convince her to marry him, realising that he could, in fact, be happy with someone other than Melissa, had been his first step to changing his life.

He wasn't going to stop just because Sophie wasn't over Nick. She had been his best chance of moving on, Bram knew, but she wasn't his only chance.

So he had gone to the pub and talked to poor Vicky Manning and tried to be positive. But it hadn't felt right. And then Sophie had rung and the mere sound of her voice had been enough to make the idea of marrying anyone else absurd.

And now here she was, her expression cross and sulky, her hair tumbling as wildly as ever around her face, her mouth set in a fiercely straight line, and he was so glad to see her that the tightness in his chest eased for the first time in a week.

They had turned off onto the narrow country road that led up to Askerby. There was very little traffic this way, but Bram pulled off the road into the entrance to a field.

Bess sat up, instantly alert, as they stopped, but Bram wasn't going anywhere, it seemed. He sat with his arms resting on the steering wheel, staring through the windscreen to where the twin beams of his headlights cut a swathe through the darkness.

'Sophie,' he said after a while. 'I'm sorry.'

She turned her head at that. 'I'm sorry too,' she said, her throat tight. 'I shouldn't have got you into this mess in the first place.'

'Well, there's no one I'd rather be in a mess with,' said Bram, and the hint of a smile in his voice made him sound like the Bram she knew once more. 'At least we're in it together. Tell me what you want to do.'

'What I really want is to rewind time, preferably to nine o'clock yesterday evening, before I started telling whopping lies to my sister,' said Sophie glumly, but she was already feeling better.

'What made you do it?'

'Oh, I don't know… I suppose I'd been thinking about our conversation last weekend. I was tired of trying to convince Melissa that she doesn't need to feel guilty any more. I wanted her to think that I really was over Nick, and she was so delighted when I told her about us that I didn't have the heart to ring her back and tell her that it wasn't true after all.

'I'm sorry,' she said. 'It seemed like a good idea at the time.'

CHAPTER FIVE

'DOES it still seem like a good idea now?' Bram asked.

'Yes...yes, it does.' Having plunged into the situation without looking—typical, her mother would say—Sophie was beginning to think that it might all work out for the best. 'It would certainly keep Mum and Melissa happy this Christmas, anyway.'

'Forget your mother and Melissa,' said Bram, who thought privately that Sophie had always been too protective of her little sister, and spent far too much time keeping her happy when she should have been thinking about herself. 'What about *you*?'

'Well, yes—me too, I suppose,' said Sophie, a little surprised. 'It would certainly be easier to face Nick if you were there. Of course it doesn't solve your problem,' she went on worriedly. 'Pretending to be engaged to me won't help you find a wife, will it?'

Bram lifted his shoulders in a resigned gesture. 'Finding a wife can wait a few weeks.'

'Then you'll help me?'

He looked at her. She had taken her seat belt off and turned in her seat to face him, her eyes shining in the darkness and her face somehow vivid through the gloom. How could he not help her? She was Sophie.

'Of course I will,' he said simply.

'Oh, thank you, thank you, thank you!' Sophie was so relieved she leant across Bess and kissed Bram impulsively on the cheek. Her lips were soft and warm against his skin, and the elusive gorse scent of her hair made Bram's senses reel for a disorientating moment.

'You are such a star!' she told him, and then sat back, laughing protestingly as Bess, reluctant to miss out on any demonstration of affection, began to lick their chins indiscriminately. 'I'll make it up to you, Bram, I promise.'

Bram wished he couldn't still feel her lips against his cheek. Lucky Bess had been there to break things up. For one terrible moment he had felt an unexpected urge to put his arm round her and pull her lush warmth closer—and then where would he have been?

Clearing his throat, he tried to steady his still spinning senses. 'If we're going to convince everybody that we really are engaged, we're going to have to do this properly,' he said.

'We don't have to do anything, do we?' said Sophie, putting her arm round Bess to calm her down. The dog subsided happily against her, panting in contentment.

Lucky Bess, Bram thought involuntarily.

And then, Where had *that* thought come from?

'Surely we just need to agree if anyone asks us if we're engaged?'

'I seem to remember getting engaged involves a bit more than that,' said Bram, thinking of his brief engagement to Melissa. It seemed like another life now. 'We'll need to go and see your parents, for a start, and make it official.'

'I know.' Sophie hunched her shoulders against the thought and her wide mouth turned down in exaggerated trepidation. 'I can't say I'm looking forward to that.'

'Have you spoken to your mother yet?'

'No,' she said guiltily. 'I wanted to talk to you first, so that we had our story straight. I made Ella answer the phone this morning, and I've had my mobile switched off all day. I'm sure she'll have been trying to ring, but I haven't dared check for messages! Has she tried to call you?'

'I don't know. I left the answer machine on and skulked around the shed in case I suddenly saw her car there when I came back at lunchtime... Not that I'm afraid of her, or anything!'

'Not much!' Sophie couldn't help laughing at the idea of Bram creeping around his own farm to avoid her mother.

'I just thought it would be better if we talked to her together,' said Bram, with a fine attempt at dignity. But the corner of his mouth was twitching. 'What do you think she'll say?'

'I think we can be sure there'll be a comment about what I'm wearing,' said Sophie, resigned to her mother's habits, 'but I would have thought she'd be pleased at the idea of us getting married. It means she'll be able to look Maggie Jackson in the eye again, if nothing else. I'm more worried about her asking a lot of personal questions we won't be able to answer. You know what she's like. I'm sure she'll catch us out.'

'We'll just keep things simple and stick with the story that you told Melissa. I fell in love with you, then you realised that you were in love with me. That's easy enough. I think the body language will be more difficult.'

'Body language? What body language?'

'Exactly,' said Bram. 'We're comfortable together as friends, but not as lovers. I remember being engaged to Melissa. When you first announce it you're the centre of attention, and I think people would notice if we weren't at ease touching each other, and they might start to wonder how much in love we really were.'

'It just means the occasional hug or kiss, though, doesn't it?' said Sophie airily. 'No one is going to expect us to go in for passionate clinches over the roast turkey. I don't mind giving you a squeeze every now and then and calling you darling! You can do that too, can't you?'

A much too vivid image of what it would be like to hold Sophie close and kiss her presented itself to Bram, and he had to make quite an effort to push away the thought of how soft and luscious she would be. There was something wrong about the way thoughts like that kept creeping up on him unawares, he decided. It made him distinctly uncomfortable.

'I expect I could manage that,' he said gruffly, and leant forward to switch on the ignition to give himself something to do. 'Let's go and see your parents, then, and break the news that we're engaged.'

'We might as well get it over with,' Sophie agreed, refastening her seat belt.

'Then what?' asked Bram as he put the Land Rover in gear and set off along the dark road. 'Do you have to go back to London?'

'Only because my things are there.' She told him about her losing her job. 'I'm not likely to get anything else before Christmas now, so it would be cheaper for me to come home, but I'm not sure how long Mum and I would last without killing each other. I love her, but she drives me crazy—and vice versa.

'And then there's the fact that Nick and Melissa are always popping in to Glebe Farm,' she went on. 'I can brace myself to see him at Dad's birthday, if I've got you there, but seeing him on a day-to-day basis would be awful. I don't think I could bear that.'

'Why don't you come and stay at Haw Gill until Christmas?' Bram suggested. 'It would look convincing, if nothing else, and you could help me on the farm.'

Sophie brightened instantly at the idea. 'Oh, that would be wonderful!' she said. 'Then all I'd need to do would be to get through Dad's party, and Christmas lunch, and then...'

She trailed off, realising that she didn't know what would happen after that.

'Yes—what then?' said Bram evenly.

'Well, then we'll break off our engagement,' said Sophie, recovering quickly. 'We can always blame Christmas. It's supposed to be very stressful on the relationship front.'

'What are we going to say? That we don't get on?'

'Obviously no one's going to believe that,' she said, ignoring the edge of sarcasm in Bram's voice. 'Besides, we don't want to end up pretending that we're not friends. No, we'll just have to say...I don't know...that we realised that getting married would be a mistake but we want to stay friends—something like that.'

'It's a bit vague.'

'I know, but I'm sure we'll be able to think of something better nearer the time,' she said. 'It's too hard to think of everything at once. Let's get through Christmas first. Then we'll find some way to call off our supposed engagement, you can start looking for a real fiancée, and maybe I can find a job up here. I don't really want to go back to London, and perhaps once I've faced Nick it'll seem easier to stay.

'Anyway, I'll worry about all that later,' Sophie finished buoyantly. 'Let's face Mum and Dad first. If we can convince Mum, we can convince anyone!'

*   *   *

As Sophie had predicted, her mother's reaction was a mixed one. Harriet was delighted at the thought of a wedding, aggrieved at not having been told their news the previous weekend, and appalled that Sophie had come to celebrate her engagement wearing torn jeans and a scruffy jumper.

'Couldn't you have put on a skirt?' she demanded. 'It's not every day you celebrate getting engaged.'

'Mum, it's cold outside!'

'Anyway, I love Sophie just the way she is,' said Bram quickly, before they could get into one of their arguments. He put his arm round Sophie and pulled her against him, smiling in what he hoped was a suitably besotted manner. 'Sophie doesn't need to dress up for me.'

Harriet sniffed a bit. 'I just hope she'll try a bit harder on her wedding day! Anyway, we're very pleased,' she said, obviously remembering that this was Sophie's day. She kissed Sophie graciously, and then Bram, who was beginning to wish he hadn't realised quite how good it felt to hold Sophie against him like that.

'Come in—your father's in the sitting room.'

Joe Beckwith was reading by the fire, but at the sight of Sophie and Bram he took off his glasses, folded his paper and got to his feet. 'So, Melissa was right, was she?' he said, kissing Sophie and shaking Bram's hand.

'I'm glad, lass,' he said simply. 'You're better off with someone like Bram than that London chap who broke your heart last year. He's lucky I never got my hands on him. But you,' he said, poking a stubby finger at Bram's chest, 'I know where to find you, so you'd better look after her!'

'I will,' said Bram. He had always liked Joe Beckwith's directness.

'It's different this time, Dad,' said Sophie, hoping that he'd never know quite how different.

Joe had no idea that the London chap who'd broken her heart was his own son-in-law, and Sophie could only pray that he would never find out. Her father would hate knowing that the man he had welcomed into the family had hurt one of his daughters as much as he had made the other one happy, and both her parents would be desperately hurt themselves to find out that the truth had been kept from them for so long.

'It had better be,' said Joe, still looking at Bram from under his bushy brows.

Harriet broke the rather awkward pause that followed by bustling in with a bottle of champagne and four elegant flutes on a tray. 'Hearing that you were engaged was just the most wonderful surprise,' she said, handing the bottle to Joe to open. 'I couldn't believe it when Melissa rang me this morning and told me. I had to make her say it twice. When did all this *happen*?'

'Just last weekend,' said Sophie, remembering the story they had agreed.

'But you were here last weekend, and you never breathed a word of it! I do think you might have told us.' Harriet sounded quite put out. 'We *are* your parents. I don't understand why it had to be a secret.'

Sophie had known it was going to be like this. She glanced rather helplessly at Bram, who took her hand in a warm clasp. 'It all happened so suddenly, Harriet,' he explained.

'Suddenly! You've known each other for years.'

'I know, but this was different,' he said. 'I've got to admit that I've been in love with Sophie for quite some time now, but I thought being friends was enough for her. And then last weekend…well, everything changed—didn't it, Sophie?'

He looked at Sophie, who smiled weakly back, impressed by how convincingly he lied. Who would have thought Bram, with his honest face and his direct blue gaze, would turn out to be such an accomplished fibber?

'It wasn't that we wanted to keep our relationship a secret from you,' Bram went on, oozing sincerity, 'but it was very new for us, and, since Sophie was going back to London, we thought that we would have the week to be sure of how we felt before we told anybody. We were planning to come and see you this weekend anyway,' he added, 'but then Melissa rang Sophie, and she just jumped the gun a bit.'

'Anyway, we're here now,' said Sophie, feeling that she should take some part in all this. 'And you're the first to know after Melissa, I promise.'

Harriet looked somewhat mollified as Joe handed out the glasses of champagne.

'Well, here's to both of you,' he said, lifting his own glass, and Harriet seconded the toast, smiling broadly.

'We're so happy for you,' she said.

'Thank you,' said Bram.

'Thanks, Mum. Thanks, Dad.' Sophie smiled at them a little awkwardly, feeling bad about deceiving them now that she could see how pleased they were for her. It was going to be awful telling them that they had broken off their engagement.

They smiled back expectantly, and the belated penny dropped—they were waiting for her to kiss Bram. Because that was the kind of thing you did when you were engaged, wasn't it?

Ah. This must be what Bram had meant by body language. Sophie remembered her breezy assurance that she would be able to manage the odd kiss without any trouble, but now that she was actually here and actually going to have to kiss Bram like a lover, not a friend, it didn't seem quite so straightforward.

It shouldn't be a problem, of course, and it would only be a little kiss, but suddenly Sophie felt as awkward as a schoolgirl.

She glanced rather shyly at Bram, who obviously had no difficulty in reading her expression, judging by the amused look in his blue eyes. He wouldn't want to kiss her particularly either, thought Sophie, but, being Bram, he didn't make a fuss. He just smiled and casually slid a hand beneath her curls so that he could cup her head and pull her towards him to drop a light kiss on her lips.

His mouth was warm and very sure. Surprisingly sure, in fact. Sophie hadn't thought that it would feel that…*right*…somehow. It felt odd to be kissing him, but at the same time it felt so comfortable, so comfort*ing*. Really, it felt very nice…more than nice…

Instinctively, she leant into the kiss. But as the pressure of his lips increased in response that feeling of comfort was dissipated by a peculiar jolt of excitement, and that didn't feel nice at all. At least, it *did*, but it didn't feel right. It felt disturbing, even dangerous, and she jerked away, her eyes wide and startled and very green all of a sudden.

'Oh, I must get my camera,' said Harriet, putting down her glass. 'Don't move!'

The kiss could only have lasted a few seconds. Bram and her father were chatting while Harriet went in search of her camera. How could they all sound so normal? Didn't they realise how odd everything felt? Sophie had the strangest sensation of having slipped into a parallel universe, where everything seemed familiar yet subtly different at the same time.

Especially Bram. Look at him, sitting there talking to her father about fencing contractors as if nothing whatsoever had happened! How could he *do* that? Hadn't he felt that sudden thrill, that unaccountable flicker of something that mere friends shouldn't feel at all?

'Here we are!' Harriet came back into the room carrying her trusty camera with which she had recorded family events for as long as Sophie could remember. 'Now, I need a picture of you two to mark your engagement.'

Harriet rather fancied herself as a photographer. In full Cecil Beaton mode, she made Sophie and Bram stand in front of the fireplace with their glasses of champagne. 'I'll just do a head shot,' she decided, tutting at Sophie's scruffy jeans. 'We don't want those in the picture!'

Fussing around Sophie, she made her take off her jumper, only to sigh at the crumpled state of the shirt she was wearing underneath. 'Don't you ever iron your clothes, Sophie?' she demanded, exasperated. 'Well, it'll have to do. It's better than that awful jumper, anyway.'

At last she was satisfied. 'Now, stand there next to Bram—and don't forget your champagne. Bram, if you could put your arm around Sophie…that's perfect.' Backing away, she picked up her camera and framed the picture. 'OK, smile!'

Sophie had rarely felt less like smiling. She was acutely aware of Bram's arm around her waist, of its hard muscle and the warmth of his hand through the fine cotton of her shirt.

'Sophie!' Harriet had lowered the camera, exasperated. 'Why are you standing awkwardly like that? Move a bit closer to Bram and do try and look relaxed. I know you hate having your picture taken, but this is your special day.'

Sighing inwardly, Sophie fixed a smile to her face and put her arm tentatively around Bram's back. It was comfortingly broad and solid—the kind of body you could lean against and feel safe.

She knew that already, of course, from the countless times she had hugged him, but for some reason it felt different to touch him now, like this. That kiss had made her feel funny, and she was aware of him in a way she had never been before.

'That's better,' said Harriet approvingly, and clicked. 'Now, I'll just do one more with a kiss.'

'Mu-um…'

'Don't make a fuss, Sophie, these are your engagement photos. You'll never have this day again, and you'll be sorry later if you don't have a proper record.' Bossily, she took away their glasses. 'Now…OK!' she called from behind the camera.

Bram's eyes met Sophie's, and his mouth quivered very slightly. 'It's easiest just to do as you're told sometimes,' he murmured as he bent his head.

At least this time she would be prepared, Sophie thought. But, even though she braced herself against it, there was nothing she could do to prevent that odd frisson of excitement—and this time it was even more disturbing, for it went hand in hand with an inexplicable feeling of not wanting the kiss to end.

Sophie felt peculiarly weightless, as if she had found herself between universes now, in a strange space where the kiss was the only thing that was real. She forgot her mother and the camera. She forgot who she was, where she was, forgot that this was her old friend Bram, and gave herself up instead to the tantalising warmth and sureness of the kiss. With a tiny sigh of pleasure, she parted her lips, and Bram's arm tightened possessively around her.

'Your mother only wants a snap, not a three-hour video.'

Joe Beckwith's dry voice jerked them apart. Brought abruptly back to his senses, Bram let Sophie go. It had felt so right to be kissing her that he had forgotten their pretence, forgotten everything except her warmth and softness and the sweetness of her kiss. Sophie herself was looking shocked again, and he hoped that she didn't think that he was taking advantage of the situation.

'Sorry,' he said, a slight flush deepening the weathered brown of his face.

'No need to apologise.' Joe sounded amused. 'If you'd been happy with a little peck on the cheek I might have been worried.' His shrewd eyes flickered between Sophie and Bram. 'Mind you, you both look a bit shellshocked. Anyone would think you'd never kissed before!'

There was a tiny silence. Sophie couldn't look at Bram. 'Don't be silly, Dad,' she said, mustering a laugh from somewhere.

Harriet put her camera down and retrieved her champagne as they all sat down at last. 'We must have a proper dinner for you,' she said, turning to Sophie, who had been feeling peculiarly boneless, especially around her knees, and was very glad to drop onto the sofa before she simply fell down.

'Melissa and Nick will want to come and celebrate your engagement too,' her mother was saying. 'What about next week?'

Sophie made a desperate effort to pull herself together. She had to forget about kissing Bram, and the strange state of her legs, and concentrate on what her mother was saying instead.

An engagement party. She should have expected something like this, Sophie thought, resigned. She was going to have to face Nick some time, of course, but next week…

'Can I let you know, Mum?' she temporised. 'I've got to go down to London to pick up all my stuff, and I don't really know when I'll be back.'

'Well, don't leave it too long. There's lots to do before a wedding, and there's not that much time before Christmas.'

Sophie stared at her mother with foreboding. 'What's it got to do with Christmas?'

Harriet didn't quite meet her eyes. 'I just happened to bump into the vicar this afternoon, and it turns out that he can fit in the ceremony on the morning of Christmas Eve,' she said. 'Of course you'll want to go and see him yourselves, but I've asked him to keep that date free for you. Perhaps you could pop along tomorrow morning just to confirm it?'

'Pop along? *Pop along?*' Sophie spluttered, so angry she could hardly get her words out. At least fury was a welcome distraction from Bram's kiss and the prospect of seeing Nick again, and a small part of her brain was busy fanning the flames deliberately. Her mother had really outdone herself this time.

'I will do no such thing! You had no business talking to the vicar, Mum. We hadn't even told you until five minutes ago, and for all you know we might not want to get married in a church.'

'Nonsense, dear. Of course you'll want to get married in church,' said Harriet, completely unfazed by Sophie's fury. 'I'm sure Molly would have wanted that for you—wouldn't she, Bram?'

Seeing Sophie about to erupt, Bram put his hand on her knee and squeezed it repressively. 'Mum always enjoyed a church wedding,' he agreed tactfully, before Sophie could speak, 'but it's not that long since she died, and in the circumstances we'd both prefer a quiet wedding.'

'Exactly,' said Sophie, with grateful glance at him. Really, Bram was much better at managing her mother than she was. 'We want to make our own arrangements.'

'Well, dear, if you insist...' Harriet assumed a hurt expression. 'But you know you're not the most organised person in the world, and it *is* normal for the bride's mother to get involved. But if you don't want me to have anything to do with the wedding, of course that's up to you. I know better than to push in where I'm not wanted.'

Sophie was practically grinding her teeth with frustration by this stage. Her mother in martyr mode was even more infuriating than when she was being bossy and overbearing.

'All I'll say—if I'm allowed to give you just a little bit of advice, that is—' Harriet went on with a touch of sarcasm '—is not to leave it all to the last minute, the way you're inclined to, Sophie. It does take a long time to plan a wedding.'

'I know that, Mum.' Sophie forced herself to stay calm. 'But we've only just got engaged. There's no reason to hurry.'

'No reason to wait either,' her father put in unexpectedly. 'It's not as if you don't know each other properly. I wasn't so happy about Melissa and Nick getting married after just a few weeks, but it would be different with you two.'

'And a Christmas wedding would be so lovely,' Harriet put in, quick to capitalise on Sophie and Bram's momentary hesitation. 'Think how romantic it would be! The church looks so pretty then, with candles, and you know how clever Maggie is with the Christmas flowers. And, of course, it would be marvellous to combine the celebrations with your father's special birthday. You'd like that, wouldn't you, Joe?'

'If that's what Sophie wants,' said her father, an old hand at not committing himself.

Feeling herself being outmanoeuvred, Sophie threw a glance of appeal at Bram. 'It all sounds very nice,' he said calmly. 'Can we have a think about it, Harriet?'

'Don't think too long. It's only six weeks until Christmas, you know, and you'll need to think about invitations, and the service you want, and the food and the flowers…oh, and a dress, of course. It can take *ages* to find exactly what you want. It's no use pretending that you can do it all at the last minute.' Glancing at her watch, Harriet got to her feet. 'I must just go and check my potatoes. You'll stay to supper, won't you? We can talk about it more then.'

'That's kind of you, Harriet,' said Bram quickly, standing as well. Sophie shot up beside him, terrified that he was going to leave her behind. She tugged discreetly at his hand. 'But *we've* got to get back, I'm afraid,' he added, obedient to the mute appeal in her eyes.

'Oh, dear… Well, if you must.'

Fortunately her parents seemed to take it for granted that Sophie would be leaving with Bram.

'You two have a talk about what you want,' Harriet was saying as she led the way to the door, 'and I'll give you a ring tomorrow. I'll talk to Melissa tonight, and we'll arrange a date for an engagement dinner with them. You can let me know what you've decided about the wedding too,' she went on as Sophie wrapped herself up in her scarf and shrugged on her jacket.

'If you want to keep things small we could always do the food here, but I know the most marvellous florist in York...'

Still talking, she accompanied them out to the Land Rover, where Bess was sitting behind the steering wheel, alert for Bram's return, and snatches of advice about finger buffets and getting invitations printed interspersed her farewell kiss to them both.

Sophie dropped her head back and sighed as Bram headed down the track. 'I'm sorry about that,' she said. 'My mother...!'

'It could have been worse,' said Bram comfortingly, and she turned to stare at him.

'How?'

'She could have whipped out a special licence and had us married off tomorrow.'

Sophie rolled her eyes. 'God, I bet she wishes she'd thought of that one!'

'She'd have prepared a finger buffet on the sly and got Maggie Jackson to do the flowers.'

'Oh, but what would she have done about a dress?' asked Sophie, getting into the spirit of it. 'I can't imagine Mum ever agreeing to me getting married in anything from my own wardrobe.'

'Hmm.' Bram pretended to think about it. 'Would she put you in Melissa's wedding dress?'

'She might if I wasn't three sizes too big for it!'

'Maybe Maggie would have let it out. *"You know how clever she is."*'

He mimicked her mother's voice so accurately that Sophie had to laugh. 'I defy even Maggie to get me into any dress of Melissa's!'

It was amazing how much better a laugh could make you feel. Some of the tension that had wound Sophie tight as her mother calmly disposed of her affairs began to seep away, and as she glanced at Bram she was conscious of a rush of affection.

'Seriously, Bram, I'm sorry about all this,' she said. 'I hope you don't mind me coming back with you, but I couldn't face a whole evening of Mum and wedding plans on my own—and now you're lumbered with me permanently, since they seem to think it's quite natural for me to move in with you.'

'At least your parents were convinced by our supposed engagement,' said Bram, turning up the track to Haw Gill. 'I thought they might be more suspicious.'

'Yes, I did too. I guess people see what they want to see.'

Her parents had looked at her kissing Bram and seen a girl in love with her fiancé because that was what they'd expected to see.

The thought of Bram's lips on hers sent a shiver of memory down Sophie's spine. How strange that feeling had been! So warm and comfortable, and yet so unexpectedly thrilling at the same time. Would it feel the same if she kissed him again?

She was suddenly desperately aware of him beside her. What would it be like to be able to reach over and put a hand on his thigh? To kiss his throat, just below his jaw? To press into his warm, solid bulk and feel safe and reassured?

Sophie could picture it all so vividly that something clenched inside her, and her involuntary sharp intake of breath in response was so loud that Bess pricked up her ears and Bram looked at her curiously as he parked the Land Rover.

'What's up?'

'Nothing,' said Sophie, but her voice sounded high and foolish.

Bram left it until they were in the kitchen. He had poured Sophie a glass of wine and was rummaging around in the fridge for something to eat. 'You know, you look a bit odd,' he said carefully. 'Is something the matter?'

'No,' she said again, wishing she could shake the memory of that kiss and go back to thinking about him with the simple affection she had felt when he had made her laugh. Instead she kept noticing the line of his back as he leant down to the fridge, the strength of his hands as he had opened the bottle of wine, the easy, unhurried way he moved around the kitchen. It made her feel jittery and uneasy, as if all the certainties that held her world together were being loosened.

Her denial sounded hollow even to herself. She took a nervous sip of wine. 'I suppose I was just thinking that we may have been *too* convincing,' she said. 'The pretence was fine, but now it's a bit like thinking it would be a good idea to drive and see what's on the other side of the hill, but now we're at the top and heading down the other side and our brakes have just failed…our vague talk of getting married one day has turned into a nightmare of engagement dinners and wedding dresses and finger buffets, and now that's all out of control too!

'You know what Mum's like,' she continued, twisting the glass between her fingers. 'We won't be able to fob her off for ever. She'll start making arrangements to-morrow, whether I ask her to or not, and then it will get harder and harder to cancel everything. If we're not careful we won't be able to stop it at all!'

CHAPTER SIX

BRAM set some cheese on the table before sitting down opposite Sophie and looking straight into her eyes, his own very blue and very direct. 'Then let's not stop it,' he said. 'Let's think about getting married.'

'We talked about this last weekend,' said Sophie, looking away from the blue gaze that was so familiar and suddenly so unsettling.

'Let's talk about it again,' said Bram. 'I'm ready to move on, forget about the past and start afresh. I think we could have a good life together. We could live here and work the farm together. You could set up a pottery in one of the old barns if you liked. At least we know we'd get on. We'd be friends, like we are now.'

'But being married is about more than being friends, isn't it, Bram?' said Sophie, choosing her words carefully. It was about sharing everything.

Including a bed.

She had always felt she could talk to Bram about absolutely anything—although now she came to think of it they had never discussed sex before. Relationships, yes. Feelings, yes. But not sex itself. It just hadn't come up between them. But there was no reason why it should be any different from talking about anything else.

Except that he had kissed her now, and *everything* felt different.

She was being ridiculous, Sophie told herself. Bram was an old friend, and even if he hadn't been they were both grown ups. She was over thirty, for heaven's sake.

So why was she dithering around like a shy schoolgirl? It wasn't as if she had ever been one of those anyway.

Sex was an issue like any other, and they needed to talk about it. It would just have been easier if they hadn't kissed. If she hadn't fantasised about crawling over him in the Land Rover. If she could stop looking at him as a man and go back to thinking of him as dear old Bram.

She cleared her throat. 'Exactly what kind of marriage are you thinking of?' she started awkwardly. 'I mean, we haven't talked about the practicalities yet.'

'What sort of practicalities?'

'Well, you know—like whether we sleep together or not,' said Sophie in a rush.

'No, we haven't talked about that yet,' Bram agreed. 'Do you want to talk about it now?'

'I'm not sure,' she said truthfully, 'but I suppose we'd better.' She hesitated, glancing at him a little shyly in spite of herself. 'What do you think? Honestly?'

Bram poured himself a glass of wine while he thought about his answer, disturbed to find how vividly he could imagine making love to Sophie.

All those years of never really seeing her at all under the shapeless clothes she wore, and now, suddenly, he was aware of her in a new and disquieting way. Suddenly he was thinking about how soft and warm she had felt when he'd held her, how her lips had felt when he'd kissed her, and what it would be like to roll over in bed and find her there.

Abruptly, he set the bottle back on the table, appalled to find that his hand was unsteady.

For the first time in his life Bram didn't think he *could* be honest with Sophie. She wanted him to tell her honestly what he thought, but he couldn't tell her that, could he?

'I wouldn't be thinking of our marriage as a temporary thing,' he said carefully instead. 'If we get married I want it to be a real commitment, so that we stay married and make a success of it. And, to be honest, I don't fancy spending the next thirty or so years as a celibate. I'd like a family too. There have been Thoresbys at Haw Gill Farm for generations, and it would be a good feeling to pass the farm onto a child of my own, but...'

'But what?'

'But I know how you still feel about Nick,' he said, shrugging. 'I wouldn't want you in my bed if you were going to be thinking about him all the time.'

Sophie flushed and looked away.

'What do *you* think?' asked Bram.

'I don't know,' she confessed. 'I think you're right. If we're going to be married, then we should be properly married.'

She imagined lying in bed next to him, imagined them turning to each other, holding each other, kissing each other. Her mouth dried and her heart slowed in a mixture of panic and excitement at the very idea of it.

She swallowed. Part of her suddenly longed to know what it would be like to make love with Bram, but the other part shied away nervously, dreading the thought of Nick's image interspersing itself between them. And what of Bram? How could she be sure that he would be thinking of her, and not imagining in his turn Melissa?

'It's just...there hasn't been anyone since Nick,' she blurted out. 'I try not to think about him, but I can't help it. Maybe when I've seen him again it'll be different. But right now I just don't know...'

'I'm not suggesting that we hop into bed right now,' said Bram as she trailed off hopelessly. 'If we do get married I would be prepared to wait until you were ready. When you felt that you were over Nick, ready to start a new relationship with me, you would just have to say.'

'Oh, great.' More flustered than she wanted to admit by the subject, Sophie resorted to sarcasm to cover up her confusion. 'And that would be *so* easy to drop into the conversation!'

She was looking pink and positively ruffled, and Bram couldn't help smiling at the sight of her, with that bright jumper and those wayward curls and the lush mouth. The feel of her lips still tingled on his. *Would* she ever get over Nick? Bram found himself hoping that he wouldn't have to wait too long.

'Maybe you won't have to say anything,' he said.

Involuntarily, Sophie's eyes flew up from her glass and found themselves locked with his blue ones. They stared wordlessly at each other for a long moment that stretched into another moment, and then another, while the kitchen clock ticked quietly into the lengthening silence.

It was Bram who tore his gaze away first. 'You don't need to think about it at all unless you're going to marry me,' he pointed out. 'You haven't even decided that yet.'

'No.' Sophie took a rather shaky sip of wine and told herself that it had just been a meeting of eyes. No need to get in a flutter about it.

She made herself think about what Bram had said about moving on instead. It was time for her to do that too. What was her alternative? To waste her life hankering after Nick, hoarding memories of how much she had loved him, looking back instead of forward?

Watching as Bram moved on without her?

No, if he was moving on she was going with him. She

An Important Message from the Editors

Dear Reader,

If you'd enjoy reading novels about rediscovery and reconnection with what's important in women's lives, then let us send you two free Harlequin® Next™ novels. These books celebrate the "next" stage of a woman's life because there's a whole new world after marriage and motherhood.

By the way, you'll also get a surprise gift with your two free books! Please enjoy the free books and gift with our compliments...

Pam Powers

Peel off Seal and Place Inside...

We'd like to send you two free books to introduce you to our brand-new series – Harlequin® NEXT™! These novels by acclaimed award-winning authors are filled with stories about rediscovery and reconnection with what's important in women's lives. These are relationship novels about women redefining their dreams.

THERE'S THE LIFE YOU PLANNED. AND THERE'S WHAT COMES NEXT.

Your two books have a combined cover price $11.00 in the U.S. and $13.00 in Canada, but are yours **FREE!** We even send you a wonderful surprise gift. You can't lose

THE EDITOR'S "THANK YOU" FREE GIFTS INCLUDE:

▶ Two BRAND-NEW Harlequin® Next™ Novels

▶ An exciting surprise gift

YES! I have placed my Editor's "thank you" Free Gifts seal in the space provided at right. Please send me 2 FREE books, and my FREE Mystery Gift. I understand that I am under no obligation to purchase anything further, as explained on the back and opposite page.

PLACE
FREE GIFTS
SEAL
HERE

▶ DETACH AND MAIL CARD TODAY! ▶

356 HDL D72K   156 HDL D73J

FIRST NAME	LAST NAME

ADDRESS

APT.#	CITY

STATE/PROV.	ZIP/POSTAL CODE

Thank You!

(HN-TL-11/05)

wasn't going to lose Bram to Vicky Manning or any-one else.

'OK,' she said, putting down her glass. 'I've decided.'

'And?'

'And I'll marry you.'

For a fleeting moment Sophie remembered saying ex-actly the same words to Nick, under very different cir-cumstances. Nick had arranged a romantic restaurant, candlelight, soft violins playing, even a rose... Didn't that indicate a lack of imagination on his part?

Sophie was shocked at the treacherous thought that had slipped in without her realising it. She hadn't been able to think of Nick's proposal before without crying, and now, suddenly, here she was being critical of it. How had that happened?

Of course she had said that she would marry him. Nick was a dream come true, and he had swept her off her feet with his good looks and his glamour and his smile that made her go weak at the knees. She hadn't been able to believe her own good luck. It had all seemed too good to be true.

As, of course, it had been in the end.

She didn't feel the same incredulous joy now, as she looked across the table at Bram, but just saying the words had lifted a weight that she hadn't known was there. The relief of making the decision felt good, she realised. It felt right.

'Let's get married,' she said again, and smiled.

Bram smiled back at her across the table. 'Let's do that,' he agreed, and reached for both her hands. 'I'm glad, Sophie,' he said.

Sophie was burningly conscious of the warmth of his fingers. 'Even knowing what a mother-in-law you're get-ting?'

He laughed. 'Even then.'

Had his laughter always lit his face like that? Had his eyes always been so blue, so engagingly crinkled at the edges? There was something startling about Bram suddenly as he laughed across the table at her, something strange and new that made her think about how it had felt to kiss him, something that made her spine clench with a disturbing awareness.

Sophie's eyes slid away from his face. 'At least I don't need to contemplate telling Mum the engagement's off the moment she's got it all organised,' she said, uncurling her fingers from his before they did anything rash like clinging tighter.

She picked up her glass, horrified to discover that her hand was shaking slightly. 'I'll tell her that she can make all the arrangements for the wedding after all—if that's OK with you, of course,' she added.

'Fine by me,' said Bram, getting up to see about finding something else for supper instead of catching her hands back. 'She's going to do it anyway,' he said as he opened the fridge once more. 'I'd let her get on with it.'

'Even if it means getting married on Christmas Eve?'

'Why not? I don't mind having the wedding then. But if you're still not sure, and Christmas is too soon for you, tell your mother you'd rather have a spring wedding.'

'No,' said Sophie, putting down her glass and making up her mind. 'This time I am sure. Let's get married at Christmas. I don't want to wait any longer.'

Sophie lay in bed in the spare room at Haw Gill and listened to the wind hurling itself across the moors. Baulked by the farmhouse, it screamed around the corners and rattled furiously at the windows, attacking the glass panes with gunshot splatters of rain.

It was a night to cuddle up to a lover, to feel warm and secure and cosy with his arms around you. Sophie thought about Bram lying just down the corridor. She thought about slipping down to his room and into bed with him, about snuggling in to his strong, hard body and feeling his arms close around her. It would be so comforting...or would it?

She remembered how he had hugged her at the foot of the staircase. 'Sleep well, Sophie,' he had said. 'And don't worry about anything. It will all work out the way it's supposed to.'

It'll all work out the way it's supposed to. That had been one of Molly's sayings. Sophie must have heard it a hundred times from one or the other of them. But how *was* it supposed to work out?

Sophie turned on her side, confused and restless. Until now she hadn't really questioned what she wanted. It had all been negative. She wanted things not to have happened. She wanted Melissa not to have come to London that day. She wanted Nick not to have fallen in love with her sister. She had wanted to wipe it all out and rewind time to when Nick was in love with *her*, to that giddy, joyous moment when he had reached for her hand across the table and asked her to marry him.

And now...now, suddenly, she wasn't sure exactly what she wanted—unless it was to feel certain again. It was as if she were back in that parallel universe, where everything seemed familiar but slightly out of kilter.

Like the way Bram had hugged her. His hugs had always been supremely comforting, but at the foot of the stairs that night Sophie hadn't felt comforted. She had felt unsettled, uneasy, uncertain.

Bram's hug hadn't made her want to lean on him for reassurance. It had made her aware of the strength in his arms, of the warmth of his body, of the bone and the muscle of him. It had made her wonder what those strong farmer's hands patting her back would feel like drifting over her bare skin.

The thought had been disconcerting, even disturbing, and Sophie had gone to her lonely bed feeling confused and dissatisfied, unsure now of who Bram was, of what she really wanted. Always before, if anyone had asked what she wanted, the answer would have been obvious. She wanted Nick back. But now…now she didn't know.

Was she just tired? Or was it just that kiss for her mother's camera? Would Bram go back to being Bram in the cold light of day? Or would he stay this uncannily familiar stranger? Was it she who had changed, or him?

Sophie distrusted herself now. She had loved Nick so desperately. Was she just looking for something to replace her feelings for him? That that would be using Bram, and she didn't want to do that. Bram was too special to play games with. Melissa hadn't meant to hurt him, but she had, and Sophie wasn't going to do the same.

She would be careful, Sophie decided. For once she wouldn't rush into things without thinking. Bram had said that he was prepared to wait until she was ready to make their relationship a physical one, and she wouldn't take that step until she was sure that she had banished Nick from her heart. Sure, too, that Bram was free of his own ghosts. She would be Bram's wife, and there would be plenty of time to get things right Sophie fell asleep on the thought

*   *   *

'Hmm, at least the kitchen is tidy,' said Sophie's mother, glancing critically around her. 'Which is more than I can say for you, Sophie. What *have* you been doing?'

'Clearing out one of the barns.' Sophie brushed a cobweb off her sleeve. 'Bram's going to buy me a kiln for Christmas.' She glowed at the thought. 'I want to start making pots again.'

She had been back at Haw Gill for a week after leaving London for good, and already it seemed like longer. To her relief, learning to live with Bram hadn't been nearly as awkward as she had feared it would be. It had taken no time at all for them to fall back into their comfortable friendship, and Sophie had begun to think that those strange muddled feelings she had had that first night had just been caused by a combination of nerves and exhaustion.

It wasn't that she never thought about what it would be like to sleep with Bram again. The truth was that she thought about it a little too much for her own comfort— especially when she was lying on her own in the spare room, with Bram only a few yards away.

Ella had been forthright in her opinion. 'So what if he's still in love with Melissa?' she had said when Sophie had tried to explain the situation. 'He'll soon forget her if he's got you. Why not enjoy yourselves? You've only got one life, Sophie. So what if it's not a fairy tale? Make your own fairy tale, and have a good time while you're at it!'

Part of Sophie longed to take her friend's advice, but it was hard to pluck up the courage to raise the issue again when Bram had reverted to his usual self. He was back to being her best friend, exactly as Sophie had wanted him to be the night they'd agreed to get married.

If the feel of those brief kisses hadn't been imprinted so vividly on her memory Sophie might have wondered if they had ever happened. She had been desperate to forget them, get back to the way they had always been, but now, perversely, she found it frustrating that Bram appeared to be able to do that so easily. She could hardly make a move when he was making it so clear that he was perfectly happy with the situation as it was.

Maybe Bram was finding it harder to deal with his own feelings than he had expected, Sophie speculated. Whatever the reason, the sleeping together issue appeared to have been shelved. Sophie was taking the coward's way out and following his lead.

She told herself that she was glad they were back to being good friends. They slept in separate rooms, and met at breakfast, and everything was fine. Sophie had thrown herself into life on the farm, helping Bram whenever he needed it and taking over most of the cooking. She spent the rest of the time clearing out the barn in readiness for the kiln Bram had promised her. It seemed a very generous present to Sophie, but he had pointed out that if she made a success of the business it would generate income for the farm.

'You know how your mother's always been keen for me to diversify,' he'd said. 'Here's my chance.'

Today Sophie's mother had lost patience and announced that she was coming over that afternoon. Now summoned in from the barn, Sophie was dutifully making tea while Bram went off with Bess to check the sheep grazing freely on the moor.

Harriet took her tea and sat down at the table. 'You should be spending a little less time on that pottery and a bit more on planning your wedding,' she said severely. 'Do you realise how little time you've got?'

'But I thought you had all that in hand?' Having agreed to a wedding on Christmas Eve, passing responsibility for the arrangements to her mother, Sophie had put the whole business out of her mind.

'There are still decisions you need to make.' Her mother started talking about the guest list, and the exact wording of the invitations, moving seamlessly on to a discussion of the advantages of just offering champagne and canapés instead of a full buffet, while Sophie nodded occasionally and let her eyes drift out of the window.

They had had the first hard frost of the year the night before, and the moor was still white and glittering in the bright light. It would be bitterly cold but invigorating up there today, and Sophie wished she was crunching over the frozen heather with Bram and Bess.

'Sophie, are you even listening?' asked Harriet in a long-suffering voice.

Sophie jerked her attention back to her mother. 'Of course, Mum. Um…just champagne and canapés…that sounds fine to me.'

'You might show bit of interest! It is your wedding.'

'Surely the important thing is that Bram and I are marrying each other,' said Sophie. 'The rest of the wedding stuff doesn't really matter, does it?'

'It matters to me,' said Harriet tartly. 'I don't want the whole village saying your father and I couldn't give you a decent wedding. As it is, it'll seem a very quiet affair compared to Melissa's. But as that's what you and Bram want…'

'I'm sure no one will care what our wedding is like.' Sophie tried to soothe her, but her mother only shook her head at her daughter's naivety.

'You've always been such a romantic,' she sighed, picking up her list to consult it once more. 'Ah, yes— the dress. Have you done anything about that yet?'

'Er, no,' said Sophie guiltily. Her fault. She had promised faithfully that she would go and find a wedding dress as soon as she could. 'I could go and have a look in York tomorrow,' she offered, to make amends.

'I'd better come with you. It's very hard to decide these things on your own.' Catching the flicker of dismay on Sophie's face, Harriet immediately assumed her best martyred expression. 'Of course if you don't *want* me to come I wouldn't dream of interfering.'

Sophie sighed, knowing that it was useless to protest. 'Of course I want you to come,' she said obediently. 'I just know how busy you are.'

'Not too busy for my own daughter's wedding!' Having got her own way, Harriet was all smiles once more. 'What a pity Melissa can't come tomorrow. I know she'd love to get involved, but she was telling me that they've got a meeting about their new catalogue.

'That reminds me,' she went on. 'I talked to Melissa about an engagement dinner for you, and they're both free this Saturday night, so we thought we'd have it then.'

Right—and what about asking her and Bram if they could make it to their own engagement dinner? Sophie toyed with the idea of saying that they were busy, but it was hard to come up with a good excuse when you lived up in the moors and everyone knew perfectly well that you hardly ever went anywhere.

The lack of a social life suited Sophie fine. She loved the nights curled up in one of the armchairs in the sitting room, reading, or sketching out possible designs, or chatting to Bram, or just watching the fire and knowing that he was there.

Anyway, she had to face Nick some time, thought Sophie fatalistically. It might as well be this Saturday. And at least Bram would be with her.

'I'll tell Bram,' she said.

'Fine by me.' Bram shrugged when she told him about it that night. He looked closely at Sophie. 'How do you feel about it, though?'

Thinking back, Sophie was surprised to realise that her first reaction to the prospect of seeing Nick again had been one of irritation rather than the instant emotional turmoil it had always caused before. The truth was that she hadn't actually thought about him that much recently. She had been too busy thinking about Bram and what her future at Haw Gill would be like.

She was still nervous about how she would react when she saw Nick again—afraid that she might succumb once more to the heady magic she had once felt at the sight of him, and afraid of not being able to conceal it if she did—but at least the thought of coming face to face with him didn't seem as unbearable as it had once done. Could it be that she was getting over him at last?

Sophie tested her heart cautiously. The pain was still there, but it wasn't as bad. 'I'm not looking forward to it,' she told Bram slowly, 'but I'll be OK. It's better to get it over and done with.'

And then, maybe, she would be able to move on.

Bram was thinking much the same thing. He hadn't counted on how distracting it would be having Sophie around the whole time. Her bright, vivid presence was familiar, and yet unfamiliar at the same time.

He found his heart catching unexpectedly at odd moments, like when he'd caught a glimpse of her striding over the moors, muffled in a shapeless coat and garish scarf, her hair blowing about her face. Or hauling the accumulated junk of generations out of that filthy barn, careless of the dirt and the dust. Standing at the range where his mother used to stand, humming tunelessly to herself as she stirred a pot. Watching the fire, legs tucked up beneath her, her face pensive and a little sad as the flames threw dancing shadows over her.

And every time he would remind himself that it was just Sophie, just his old friend, the same girl he had known for years without once wondering what it would be like to peel off those layers and pull her down beside him. Now he wondered all the time.

He would never know as long as Sophie was consumed by thoughts of Nick, though, and Bram found himself hoping that when she finally came face to face with him again she would discover that her love for him was not quite as strong as she remembered it.

He often wondered whether his own love for Melissa was based on a wonderful memory rather than the reality of her as a woman. With Melissa it was hard to get past her beauty to the person underneath. Bram couldn't remember what Melissa was really like. He wasn't sure that he had ever known. All he remembered was how dazzled he had felt when he was with her.

But now…now he didn't know how he felt. The only thing Bram *was* sure of was that Sophie was his friend. It was easier—safer—to revert to being 'just good friends' than to risk spoiling the friendship they had by thinking too much about what it would be like if they were something more than friends.

In any case, there was no point in thinking about it, Bram told himself, until Sophie was over Nick—and that might still be a very long time. In the meantime, he would stick to being her good friend and he would stop looking at her mouth, or the curve of her shoulder, or the inviting hollow at the base of her throat…

He would try, anyway.

*   *   *

Sophie's mother picked her up the next morning and drove with her usual efficiency to the Park and Ride outside York, so that they could get the bus right into the city centre. Cars were banished within the city walls, and Sophie had often enjoyed strolling along the old streets without having to worry about the traffic.

Not today, though. Her mother was on a mission. Having done her research for Melissa's wedding, she bore Sophie off towards a bridal shop in the maze of twisting streets at the heart of the city. 'I've made an appointment,' she said. 'They were so helpful over Melissa's dress that I'm sure we'll be able to find you the perfect wedding dress.'

'I've found it,' said Sophie, stopping dead and staring.

The dress was so stunning that it had been given the window to itself. Cut low over the shoulders and close around the waist, it fell in a flurry of chiffon layers in gold and copper and bronze and red. It glowed like a flame, so warm and so vibrant you could almost hold out your hands and warm yourself on its richness and its colour.

Sophie took one look at the dress and fell in love with it. Now, *there* was a dress to be married in—a dress that would make you feel joyous and sexy and vibrant. Surely the way you should feel when you were getting married. Even if it was to an old friend who was still in love with your sister.

Still talking, Harriet had walked on some way before she realised that Sophie wasn't with her. Backtracking, she tutted her annoyance. 'We'll be late.'

'Look.' Sophie pointed. 'There's my wedding dress.'

Her mother looked. 'That's not a wedding dress, Sophie,' she said with distaste. 'It's *red*!'

'There's no law that says wedding dresses have to be white, is there?

'I was thinking more of ivory,' said Harriet. 'You have been living together, after all, and white wouldn't be flattering to you. You're too sallow.'

'This dress would be flattering,' said Sophie, knowing without even trying it on that it was a dress made for her.

But her mother wasn't having any of it. 'Whatever would people think if you went up the aisle in that? A red dress like that is *quite* inappropriate for a church.'

Well, what did it matter really? Sophie asked herself with a last longing look at the dress as her mother dragged her on. It wasn't as if it would be a real wedding. She and Bram were entering into a marriage of convenience. If they were just going through the motions what difference would a dress make?

So she let herself be swept into the bridal shop, where she stood and was measured and eyed up while her mother consulted with the immaculate assistants. After a lot of discussion they settled on a very simple dress in ivory silk. It had long chiffon sleeves and a sweetheart neckline, with a tight bodice from which the skirt fell in elegant folds to the floor. Even Sophie had to agree that it was beautiful, and very flattering, but it didn't make her feel the way she knew the flame-coloured dress would have done.

'How did you get on?' Bram asked her when she got in that evening. He had started making the supper, and had been trying not to think about how empty the kitchen felt without her, when Sophie burst through the door and collapsed into a chair by the fire with an exaggerated sigh of relief.

'I'm exhausted!' she told him. 'I've been run over by

my mother's will so many times today that I'm surprised I can stand up at all! I was very good, though. I did as I was told and I'm going to look the perfect conventional bride—complete with long white dress, matching shoes and a tiara. You'll be glad to know that I drew the line at a veil. But, oh, Bram! I saw the perfect dress.'

She told him about the dress that had made her think of a flame. 'You know I'm not much of a girl for dresses,' she said, 'but that was a dress that would make you feel a million dollars.'

'It sounds like the kind of dress you should have,' said Bram.

'Well, I've agreed on the traditional one now,' said Sophie, resigned. 'I couldn't afford to buy it myself anyway, and it probably wasn't suitable to get married in. But it was so beautiful!'

She got up and began laying the table, and Bram said no more, but when he got back from feeding the stock the next morning he asked her if she had any plans for the day.

'Not really,' said Sophie. 'We could do with some more shopping, so I might do a supermarket run, but apart from that I was just going to carry on with the barn.'

'We'll do the supermarket on the way back,' said Bram.

'Back from where?'

'We're going to York.'

'But I was only there yesterday,' Sophie objected. 'What do you want to go for?'

'We're going to get you that dress,' said Bram.

CHAPTER SEVEN

'COME on,' he said, after one look in the window the next morning. 'You're going to try it on.'

'We don't even know how much it costs,' said Sophie feebly. 'It's probably terribly expensive.'

But Bram was already inside the shop. An assistant who couldn't have been more than a size six was despatched to find a dress in Sophie's rather larger size. Her gaze had flickered dismissively over Sophie, in her jeans and bulky jumper, but had lingered with more interest on Bram.

When Sophie was in the changing cubicle she could hear the assistant chatting up Bram outside. Some girls had no shame, she seethed inwardly. And Bram ought to know better than to encourage her. He was an engaged man. He had no business flirting back and giving the impression that his options were still open.

Sophie's lips tightened jealously as she unzipped her jeans and pulled off her jumper, but it was impossible to stay cross when she stepped into the dress.

It slithered over her, clinging in all the right places and swinging and swirling away in the ones you were less keen to draw attention to. The material was whisper-soft, its touch like a caress against her bare skin, and the colour was like a shout of joy. Standing there in her bare feet, without a scrap of make-up, Sophie felt incredibly sexy, even powerful in that dress.

Pushing open the cubicle door, she stepped out, and Bram and the assistant fell abruptly silent.

'What do you think?' asked Sophie, losing her assurance with every second that the silence lengthened. Were they trying to think of a polite way to say that she was much too fat for a dress like this?

Bram swallowed. 'We'll take it,' he said to the assistant, without taking his eyes off Sophie. She looked incredible, warm and vibrant and voluptuous, the rich colour making her skin glow and throwing the clear grey eyes and the tangle of dark curls into relief.

The assistant's glance was more critical, but there was surprised approval in her expression too. 'She'll need shoes,' she said, suddenly coming to life. 'Let me see what I can find.'

She was back a few minutes later with a selection of high-heeled shoes which she made Sophie try on with a firmness worthy of Harriet.

'I can't possibly walk in those,' Sophie protested, and then stopped as she saw the pair the assistant was lifting out of the box. 'Oh,' she said on a long, drawn out breath.

They were a coppery colour, with a frivolous peep toe and a floppy bronze bow on the side. Sophie slipped them on, teetering slightly at the unaccustomed height of the heel, and did a little pirouette. The chiffon layers swirled and floated around her and she smiled at the sheer silliness of the shoes and the sensuous feel of the dress. She was still smiling as she spun back to meet Bram's eyes.

The expression in them made her heart stumble, and she faltered inelegantly on her heels, unable to do more than stare dumbly back at him as her smile faded. Her heart was slamming suddenly, painfully against her ribs, and her lungs hurt until she realised that she had forgotten to breathe and gulped in some oxygen.

Bram was having trouble with his own breathing. In, out. In, out. He had never had any difficulty with it before, but the sight of Sophie spinning slowly, smiling, had caught him totally unprepared. He was used to her bundled up in the shapeless jumpers and trousers she usually wore. He couldn't remember the last time he had seen her in a dress—Melissa's wedding, probably—but even in his wildest fantasies he hadn't known that she could look like this: alluring, gorgeous, deeply sexy.

He hadn't known that he could want her so much.

He hadn't known that he could love her so much.

Of *course* he loved her. Bram looked at Sophie and knew that she could never again be just his friend. It was a strange feeling to fall in love with someone you already loved—a bit like putting in the last bit of a jigsaw, standing back and being able to see at last how all the pieces made sense when they were put together.

That was how it was with him. He still loved Sophie as a friend, but he wanted her as a woman—wanted her with a fierceness and an urgency that shook him out of his habitual steady practicality and left him floundering.

He hadn't loved Melissa like this. Melissa was someone to be adored, so fragile, so lovely, that you feared she might dissolve into a dream if you reached out for her. But Sophie—Sophie was a real, warm, earthy woman for loving. She was a woman you could touch and hold and laugh with, a woman you could get down and dirty with, a woman to share your life with.

As the last certainties about how he felt about Sophie fell away, Bram felt as if he had missed his step and fallen off a cliff. He was still falling, still struggling desperately to get a grip, when he realised belatedly that Sophie and the assistant were looking at him with identical curious expressions.

'Bram?' said Sophie in concern.

'We'll—' His voice seemed to belong to someone else entirely. Bram cleared his throat and tried again. 'We'll take the shoes as well,' he said.

'Where now?' he asked as they emerged from the shop, armed with a huge paper carrier bag.

'Lunch?' suggested Sophie, pushing aside the memory of her mother's lecture on her need to lose weight before the wedding. Yesterday she had actually made her have a salad for lunch, in spite of Sophie's objections that it was a freezing winter day.

Bram made a huge effort to pull himself together as they set off in search of a café, but it was hard with Sophie swinging along beside him, and when all he wanted to do was pull her into a doorway and kiss her until she told him that she loved him too, that she wanted him as badly as he wanted her, that she didn't care about Nick any more.

But Bram didn't think Sophie would say that, no matter how hard he kissed her.

Sophie was enjoying herself. It was much more fun being with Bram than with her mother. York was looking at its best, and it was lovely to have the time to wander, looking at the quirky details of the buildings, peering down alleyways and watching the street performers. The Christmas lights were up, and there were decorations in almost every window, while a cacophony of Christmas music spilled out of shops, one song blurring into another as they passed.

Bram did seem a bit tense, though. Sophie was afraid he might be regretting the expense of the dress and the shoes—she certainly would be if she had had to fork out that kind of money—but that wouldn't be like him. He was always so sensible, so practical about everything.

He wouldn't buy anything that he couldn't afford, and he certainly wouldn't regret his generosity, or show it if he did. He wasn't that kind of man.

She eyed him in concern as he stopped to peer at a display of antique jewellery, rubbing his jaw thoughtfully, his face intent. He studied the shop window exactly the same way he'd study a truculent ewe during lambing, Sophie thought, watching him with affection.

As if aware of her gaze, Bram turned his head and smiled at her, and she was conscious of a stab of happiness so sharp that it made everything seem suddenly vivid: the lines around his eyes, the crease in his cheek, the weight of the carrier bag in her hand. It was as if the world itself had snapped into focus, with every brick and stone clearly outlined, every paving slab beneath her feet smooth and solid, every sense in her body alert.

When was the last time she had felt this alive? Sophie wondered. Not since Nick, and even then her joy had been tinged with disbelief. She had thought that she would never be truly happy again.

Now here she was, standing in a York street with her oldest friend, while the quartet playing 'Silent Night' at the end of the street competed with the strains of 'I Saw Mommy Kissing Santa Claus' blaring from the gift shop opposite, and she realised she was happy—truly happy.

She smiled at Bram.

'What?' he asked.

'Oh…nothing,' she said, not sure she could explain.

Bram turned back to the window. 'You should have an engagement ring.'

Instantly Sophie's unclouded happiness vanished in a flurry of guilt. 'You've already spent far too much money on me,' she protested. 'And you can't claim this dress as part of the farm assets! I don't need a ring, honestly.'

'You should have one,' Bram repeated stubbornly. 'Your mother and Melissa would expect it. Do you like that one?'

He pointed to an antique ring, the fine rubies interset with pearls. Reluctantly Sophie came to stand beside him, and leant closer to follow the line of his finger. Bram felt her hair brush his cheek as she craned her head, and the impulse to pull her into his arms was so strong that he stiffened and made himself step abruptly away.

Sophie felt him jerk away from her and straightened awkwardly, feeling as if she had overstepped an invisible boundary and invaded his personal space. A faint flush stained her cheeks. 'Sorry,' she muttered.

'No, it was me…I'm sorry,' said Bram uncomfortably.

They both stared desperately at the window, very conscious of the silence heavy with a new constraint.

Bram could have kicked himself for his instinctive recoil. He could tell that Sophie was rather hurt, but he couldn't explain why he had pulled away like that. Telling her that he loved her, that he was afraid he might lose control of his feelings and grab her in the open street just hours before she had to face the love of her life for the first time in over a year, was hardly guaranteed to make the atmosphere more comfortable, was it?

'Well, what do you think?' he asked instead.

'It's lovely,' said Sophie, passionately grateful to him for breaking that awkward pause. 'But look at the price! You could buy a bull for that!'

Bram couldn't help smiling at her logic. 'We don't

need another bull,' he pointed out. 'Why don't we go in and see if it fits?'

It was perfect. Cinderella must have felt the same uncanny sense of rightness as the glass slipper had been slipped onto her foot. The ring sat on Sophie's hand as if it had been made for her finger.

'Do you like it?' asked Bram.

'I love it,' she said honestly, turning her hand to admire the deep glow of the rubies against the cool lustre of the pearls, bound together with warm old gold in an unusual, asymmetrical setting. 'It's different, isn't it? But that's what makes it special.'

'Like you.'

Bram had turned away to find his credit card, and he spoke so quietly that Sophie wasn't sure if she had been meant to hear or not.

She might not have heard properly anyway. Bram might have been saying thank you to the jeweller. It might have been that. Better to pretend she hadn't heard at all, she decided.

Once, she wouldn't have hesitated to dig Bram in the ribs and ask him what he had said. *What do you mean, like you?* she would have been able to demand, and Bram would have been able to tell her to mind her own business or to get her ears syringed. *I wasn't talking to you,* he would have said with a grin. *What makes you think* you're *special?*

And Sophie would have just laughed, knowing that she was his best friend and so of course she was special. She would have hugged him and told him not to be such a grump.

But she couldn't do any of those things now. Not now that he had kissed her. Not now that she knew how warm and sure his lips were, how her senses shivered at the

idea of kissing him again. And especially not now that
he had leapt away from her closeness in a way he would
never have done before, as if he couldn't bear to touch
her.

No, best ignore it, thought Sophie. If Bram wanted
her to know that he thought she was special, he would
tell her directly. She was just letting her imagination
carry her away. They were still friends. A little kiss
shouldn't have changed that. All she had to do was treat
Bram the way she always had.

So when they got up to go she hugged him. 'Thank
you, Bram,' she said, with a bright smile—the kind of
smile you would give to someone who was a generous
friend and nothing more. 'It's a beautiful ring.'

Again there was that tell-tale moment of hesitation
before his arms closed tightly around her to hug her
back. He held her so firmly that Sophie felt a sudden
urge to lean into his hard body and cling to him, to tell
him that she felt confused and unsure about everything
and to beg him not to let her go.

But friends didn't do that kind of thing, did they? So
she pulled back quickly and put her smile back in place.

'So, what about that lunch?'

They found a restaurant in a wonderful old building
with sloping floors and wonky walls, where the fires
were lit in the grates and the tables were full of
Christmas shoppers pulling presents out of carrier bags
and comparing their purchases. Sophie watched two
women at the next table, happily striking names off their
Christmas lists and urging each other to have a glass of
mulled wine with their lunch, and wished that all she
had to think about was the perennial problem of what to
buy *her* father for Christmas.

Instead of thinking about how she could want to cling

to Bram and be in love with Nick at the same time. If she *was* still in love with Nick. But if she wasn't, why would she be so nervous about seeing him tonight?

It seemed to Sophie that she had been carrying round the loss of Nick's love like a dead weight in her heart for so long now that it had become familiar, more familiar than actually loving him. The image of Nick himself had blurred over time, leaving her only the memory of how desperately she had loved him, how torn she had been between loving him and loving her sister, and the raw, terrible pain of giving him up for Melissa.

Was it that blurring that was making her so unsettled, so uneasily aware of Bram and so confused now about what she really wanted?

She glanced across the table at Bram. He was studying the menu, his eyes lowered, so her gaze could dwell on the familiar features and the cool, quiet lines of his cheek and his mouth. Watching him, Sophie was suddenly swamped by that vertiginous feeling again, as if she were standing on the edge of an abyss, desperately searching for something safe and familiar to cling to.

But the more she looked, the less safe and familiar Bram seemed. It's Bram—it's *Bram*, she kept telling herself. Strong, caring, steady Bram. Only now that strength and steadiness seemed all at once exciting and intriguing and inexplicably out of reach. Sophie remembered how he had recoiled from her touch, his hesitation before hugging her, and a desolate voice deep inside reminded her that she was just his friend. She was there to talk to, to laugh with, but not to touch.

So *be* his friend, Sophie told herself fiercely. They had been friends for as long as she could remember, and the thought of that friendship fading into awkwardness was unbearable. Much better to stay friends and forget about the comfort of touching him, forget about the feel of his lips.

Bram looked up from the menu. His eyes, so blue, so direct, made Sophie's heart turn over. 'Well, have you decided?' he asked.

'Yes,' she said, not bothering to look at the menu. Sophie knew they would always be friends and anything more would be a bonus. 'Yes, I have.'

So she smiled and chatted through lunch, and all that afternoon, until the pale wintry sunshine began to fade and the lights glowed in the shop windows and sparkled in the street decorations overhead. Super-cheerful, super-friendly, Sophie made sure they kept moving so that there was no time to think. She found Christmas presents for the family, and a special birthday present for her father, and last of all they ordered wedding rings to be engraved with the date of their marriage.

'Oh, a Christmas wedding!' exclaimed the assistant when she saw the date. 'How romantic!'

'If only she knew!' Sophie whispered to Bram as they left the shop. She rolled her eyes in amusement, behaving exactly the way she would have behaved if she hadn't been trying so hard, she thought.

Bram wasn't helping, though. The more cheerful and friendly Sophie tried to be, the more distant he seemed to become. And now, when he was supposed to laugh, to show that he understood the absurdity of the situation, all he did was look at her blankly.

'Knew what?'

'You know…the real reason why we're getting married.' Sophie was beginning to wish that she hadn't said anything. 'I'm just saying she probably wouldn't think it was quite so romantic.'

'You mean if she knew that we were both settling for second best?' said Bram, in a hard voice.

'Well…yes.' Sophie hadn't wanted to put it quite that way—but then, how else *could* you put it?

'You can make anyone believe anything if the trappings are right,' he agreed, expressionless. 'It's all about appearances.'

'Let's hope that it works tonight, then,' said Sophie, hearing the brittleness in her own voice but unable to do anything about it. She had the awful feeling that the conversation was going in quite the wrong direction, like a runaway train heading for a broken bridge, but she couldn't seem to turn it round and send it back onto safe ground.

'Tonight?'

She lifted her hand to show the pearl and ruby ring. 'This is the ultimate trapping, isn't it? If this doesn't convince Nick that we really are getting married, nothing will.'

No, and convincing Nick was what this was all about, wasn't it? Bram reminded himself. Sophie had already had an engagement ring that had meant something to her. Of course she would think of his ring as a mere 'trapping'.

'I suppose Nick bought you a diamond?' he said disparagingly.

'He did, as a matter or fact.'

'What happened to it?'

'I gave it back to him,' said Sophie, shivering in her jacket. The darkness had brought a new intensity to the cold and she turned up her collar against the icy wind.

It hadn't been the biggest ring in the world, but at the time she had been so thrilled and ecstatic at the evidence of Nick's love for her that she wouldn't have changed it for the Koh-i-Noor.

Bram remembered her face when she had told him how in love she was with Nick, and felt ashamed of his jealousy. Of course she was going to have treasured Nick's ring more than the one she was wearing now.

'I'm sorry, Sophie,' he said, more gently.

Hunching his shoulders in his jacket, he looked away. 'Look, have you done enough? It's time we headed back.'

Preferably to the way they had been for the last few days.

The journey back to Haw Gill was a silent one, and it was dark by the time they arrived. Bram went out to check on the stock, accompanied by an ecstatic Bess, who'd hated being left behind all day.

In the farmhouse, Sophie couldn't settle. She wandered around touching things, picking them up and putting them down again uncertainly. The ring on her finger kept catching her eye, reminding her about the deception they had embarked upon so carelessly.

Had she done the right thing in deciding to marry Bram? It had seemed to make sense, but now she wasn't so sure. And it was getting harder and harder to put a stop to the wedding preparations. In a couple of hours they had to turn up at the engagement dinner her mother had planned so carefully and play the happy couple in front of her family.

And Nick.

After dreading seeing him for so long, Sophie found herself strangely eager to come face to face with him now. Surely when she saw him again she would know how she really felt about him, and she would feel less confused about everything?

She took her time getting ready. She had a bath, washed her hair, and did her best to comb her wild curls into some kind of style. To keep her mother quiet she even put on some lipstick. Cutting off the labels, she put on the dress and the shoes, and found a pair of Ella's more dramatic creations to hang in her ears. There was something about this dress, Sophie thought, regarding her reflection. She felt better, stronger, more confident already.

Walking very carefully on her heels, she made her way downstairs. Bram had already changed and was waiting for her at the bottom. Unaccustomed to wearing a jacket and tie, he was running a finger around his collar, but he froze as he saw Sophie.

She looked beautiful—even more beautiful than she had in the shop. Bram wasn't sure exactly what she'd done to look so different, but she had clearly made a huge effort. No prizes for guessing why, he told himself bitterly. She would want Nick to realise just what he had lost—want Melissa to think that she had moved on and had no regrets.

'You look great,' he said as Sophie reached the bottom of the stairs, but his voice was strangely flat.

'Thanks.' She smiled a little nervously, and he saw the doubt clouding the beautiful grey-green eyes. 'I don't feel like me at all,' she confessed.

Bram studied her. In that dress she looked vibrant and sexy and faintly tousled, as if she had just fallen out of bed. Very sexy, in fact.

'I think you look exactly like you,' he said, and then made the mistake of looking into her eyes. Finding himself trapped in the river-coloured gaze, seeing it widen, he could only stare back at her for a long, long moment while his chest tightened with the longing to reach for her and sweep her into his arms.

It seemed an age before he could wrench his eyes away. Think, Bram, he told himself. Say something. Anything.

'Are you going to be all right tonight?' It was the first thing that came into his head.

'I'll be fine,' said Sophie, who was feeling none too steady herself. 'I think I'm ready to see Nick now.' She managed a smile and tried to explain. 'I'm even looking forward to it, in a funny kind of way.'

Bram's only option was to make a joke of it. 'Sure you don't want me to stay here? I wouldn't want to cramp your style!'

'No.' Sophie shook her head so that the curls bounced around her face, and came forward to tuck her hand in his arm. 'I need you with me,' she told him, sinkingly aware of how tense his muscles felt beneath her hand. This wasn't going to be an easy evening for Bram either.

'How about you?' she asked.

'Me?'

'Melissa will be there,' she reminded him gently. 'I know it's a difficult situation for you too.'

Her warm body was pressed against him, her fingers on his arm, her eyes searching his face with concern. She was close enough for him to smell the clean gorse smell of her hair, close enough to kiss.

'More than you can possibly know,' he said, his voice as dry as dust.

A smart new BMW was parked outside Glebe Farm when they arrived. Nick and Melissa were there already.

Bram put the Land Rover next to the other car and switched off the engine. Sophie had been silent on the drive over, and he thought she must be nervous about seeing Nick now that the moment was here. Reaching over, he took her hand.

'OK?'

Sophie looked down at their linked hands. She could feel the warmth of his clasp flowing up her arm, steadying her insensibly. Nick was only yards away and she was longing to stay here, holding hands with Bram in the dark. Bram, who must be dreading this evening as much as she was. She might have to face Nick, but Bram had to see Melissa being happy too.

At least she and Bram were friends. Sophie clung to the resolution she had made in York. Together they would get through this evening, and then they could go back to Haw Gill and it would just be the two of them again.

'Yes.' She took a deep breath and turned to Bram. 'Yes,' she said more strongly. 'I'm fine.'

The front door opened just then, and Sophie's mother stood outlined in a rectangle of yellow light. 'We'd better go,' said Bram.

He opened his door and got out. 'It's pretty muddy out here,' he said. 'You'll ruin those shoes. Wait there.' Squelching round to the passenger door, he held out his arms with a grin. 'Come on, I'll carry you. Just one more service I offer!'

Something about his smile made Sophie feel strange. 'You can't carry me,' she protested. 'I'm much too heavy!'

'You're not heavier than that heifer I was dragging around the other day,' Bram pointed out. 'Now, stop arguing. You know your mother will never let you hear the end of it if you turn up with muddy shoes,' he added cunningly.

That was only too true. Sophie wriggled out onto the step and linked her arms around Bram's neck, so that he could lift her easily in his arms and push the door shut with his foot.

She was burningly aware of his body as he held her against him and carried her over to set her down on the doorstep in front of Harriet. The whole thing lasted only a few seconds, but Sophie felt cold and bereft when he let her go. It was hard to concentrate on greeting her mother when the feel of his arms was branded on her flesh, making her tingle all over—which was a pity, really, as she couldn't properly appreciate the fact that Harriet was actually approving of her appearance for once.

'You look very nice, dear,' she said, kissing Sophie. 'See what you can do when you make an effort?'

She ushered them into the sitting room, where the conversation broke off abruptly as Sophie appeared with Bram by her side. Well aware that no one was looking at him, Bram was able to study the varying expressions of the others as they stared at Sophie.

Joe Beckwith looked amazed and proud, Melissa surprised and delighted, and Nick simply stunned.

It was Joe who recovered first. 'You look gorgeous, love,' he said, kissing Sophie. 'What happened to you?'

'It must be love...or maybe it's just the new dress,' said Sophie lightly, astounded at how normal she sounded.

She turned to her sister, as exquisite as ever in a classic little black dress of the kind Sophie would never be able to wear. 'Hello, Mel,' she said.

'Oh, Sophie, it's lovely to see you!' Melissa hugged her tightly. 'Dad's right—you look *beautiful*!'

Sophie laughed, a little embarrassed by all the attention. 'I don't think anyone would say that when I'm standing next to *you*!'

'Yes, they would,' said Melissa loyally.

She was right, Bram thought. Sophie would never have her sister's perfect beauty, but she was so vivid, aglow in the flame-coloured dress, that next to her Melissa looked unusually dim.

Melissa looked past Sophie and her lovely face brightened as she caught sight of Bram, who had been waiting, unsurprised that all the attention was riveted on Sophie.

'Bram!' Throwing her arms round him, she kissed him impulsively. 'I'm so, *so* happy for you!'

Sophie's heart ached for Bram. It must be awful for him, having the woman he loved in his arms, pressed closed against him, but being unable to do more than kiss her like a brother. No wonder he had been tense in York. He had probably been dreading seeing Melissa again as much as she was dreading Nick.

She saw his arms close around Melissa, and his head bent to return her kiss, but she couldn't read his expression—

'And here's Nick,' her father prompted, obviously surprised by the way Sophie was ignoring her brother-in-law.

With a start, Sophie turned away from the embrace between Bram and Melissa to greet Nick.

Nick, the love of her life. Nick, the beat of her heart for so long.

For how long had she dreaded this moment, expecting to feel jolted, desolate, yearning still? And now it was here her heart was quite steady, and more than half her attention was on Bram and what he might be saying to Melissa.

'Hello, Nick,' she said.

CHAPTER EIGHT

'Sophie, you look stunning!' said Nick, in the deep
voice that had once turned her knees to water. He gave
her a lingering kiss, slightly too close to her mouth for
comfort, and she pulled abruptly back out of his embrace.

He was just the same. The same dark good looks, the
same daredevil arrogance, the same smouldering eyes
that swept appreciatively over her curves. Alpha man
incarnate. Her heart should be thumping, her pulse rac-
ing, every nerve should be thrilling at his nearness.

But they weren't. Sophie couldn't believe it. She ex-
amined his face, waiting for the familiar rush of excitement to kick in, but there was nothing—only a curiosity
that the memory of how she had felt should be so much
stronger than what she was actually feeling now.

'I have to say my jaw just about hit the floor when
you came in,' Nick was saying, letting his eyes run appreciatively over her. 'You certainly don't look like a
farmer's wife—or farmer's fiancée, should I say?—in
that dress! I gather congratulations are in order?'

'Thank you,' said Sophie, not sure what else to say.

It was a peculiar feeling. Nick seemed the same, she
thought that she was the same, and yet somehow everything was completely different.

Sophie didn't understand how it had happened, but
her muscles, tensed for the anticipated strain of meeting
him again, were relaxing, and she was conscious of a
sense of release at the thought that the feelings that had

consumed her for so long—the love and the pain and the longing—might actually have evaporated when faced with the reality of Nick once more.

She glanced over at Bram, wanting him to know that she really was OK, but he was talking to Melissa and didn't notice her.

'Bram's a lucky man,' said Nick, following her gaze. 'He's obviously got a taste for the Beckwith sisters,' he went on, amused. 'I understand he wanted to marry Melissa at one time?'

'Yes, they were engaged for a while,' said Sophie, wondering what Bram and Melissa were talking about so intently together.

Her parents were fussing around with glasses and nuts in the background, but they hardly seemed to notice them. Melissa had her hand on Bram's arm, and her heartbreakingly lovely face was turned up to his, but they were standing so that Sophie couldn't read their expressions.

Part of her was glad that she couldn't. She didn't want to see the yearning she was afraid might show on Bram's face.

'It was a long time ago, though,' she told Nick, her eyes still on Bram, trying to interpret his body language. There was something protective about the way he was leaning towards Melissa, wasn't there? 'They were both very young.'

Her mother had already decorated the room for Christmas, and it looked warm and inviting with the lights on the tree and candles on the mantelpiece. There was even a bunch of mistletoe hanging from the light in the centre of the room. Bram and Melissa were standing almost exactly beneath it. Sophie hoped neither of them would notice.

'And you don't mind?'

Sophie brought her attention back to Nick with an effort. She frowned. 'Mind? Mind what?'

'You don't mind that Bram's one of Melissa's...how can I put it? *Cast-offs* sounds a bit crude, doesn't it?' said Nick. 'But you know what I mean.'

Sophie flushed at his tone. 'That's not how I think of Bram at all!'

'Oh, I know you've always been very fond of him,' said Nick indulgently, 'but I have to confess to being a *little* bit surprised when I heard the news.'

'Why?' she asked with a challenging look.

A smile played around Nick's mouth as he looked down into her face. 'Let's just say that I didn't think that Bram was *quite* your type,' he said softly. 'I know Melissa's still got a very soft spot for him, and he's a nice chap, but not really exciting enough for you, I wouldn't have thought. You were always so refreshingly passionate, Sophie.'

His eyes looked into hers, and she knew that he was remembering how extravagantly she had adored him. 'I can't see a sturdy hill farmer like Bram giving you what you need.'

'Can't you? I think that indicates a lack of imagination on your part, Nick.' Sophie was beginning to get angry. He was patronising Bram, and she didn't like that. 'Bram gives me just what I need, he is exactly my type—and, as it happens, I find him *very* exciting.'

'I stand corrected,' said Nick, but his smile reeked of disbelief. 'And of course I'm very glad for you. Melissa and I have been very distressed to think that you were taking so long to get over our relationship. I know how hard it was for you.'

'Do you?' said Sophie.

All the agonies she had suffered for this man, all the tears, all the homesickness because of him—and for what? Sophie looked at Nick and wondered if she had ever really known him. Had she just been consumed by a physical passion, by the joy of loving, or had she really loved the man himself? And, if it *was* Nick, what was it about him that she had loved? It was becoming very hard to remember now.

She had dreaded this moment for so long, and now that it was here she felt foolish more than anything else. Foolish and sad—for the dream she had clung to for so long and for so little point.

Nick was still musing on Sophie's relationship with Bram. 'Of course it's taken a very long time for Bram to get over Melissa, too, so you've got that in common. There's a certain symmetry to it all in a way, isn't there?' he said, with a teasing smile. 'Nothing like keeping it all in the family!'

'I don't know what you mean,' said Sophie coldly.

'I think it's very sensible of you both to make the best of things and throw in your lot together,' Nick explained kindly.

Sophie's heart sank. That was, in fact, what she and Bram were doing, but she didn't feel like sharing that with Nick right now. She should have known that he would guess. If he passed on his suspicions to Melissa her sister would always feel guilty and unhappy.

'Is that what Melissa thinks we're doing?' she asked carefully.

'No, Melissa's convinced you and Bram are love's sweet dream. She believes it because she wants to believe it.'

'You don't think it could be because she knows Bram and me better than you do?' Sophie enquired tightly, but

Nick only laughed and put an arm round her to squeeze her shoulders.

'No need to look so fierce, Sophie,' he said as she shook herself free. 'Your secret's safe with me.'

'What's all this about secrets?' Melissa asked, catching the last couple of words as she and Bram joined them.

'Nothing,' said Sophie, pink with annoyance. She glanced at Bram, wondering if he had seen her pull free from Nick's embrace, but his face was expressionless.

'It's a secret between Sophie and me,' Nick answered his wife smoothly. 'And there's no use asking, darling. That's the thing about secrets. You can't tell them.'

Sophie thought there was something mechanical about Melissa's smile, but in any case Nick gave her no time to reply. He was turning to Bram and holding out his hand.

'It's good to see you again, Bram,' he said, all easy charm. 'Congratulations! You're a lucky man.'

Bram's eyes flickered to Sophie's face. 'I know,' he said, shaking hands briefly.

'I think I'm the lucky one,' said Sophie, determined to show Nick just how wrong he was about her and Bram.

Even if he wasn't.

With a dazzling smile, she slipped an arm around Bram's waist and leaned into him. She was half afraid that he might jump away, the way he had in front of the shop window, but, after a pause so fractional that only she could have noticed it, he pulled her closer, so she was able to reach up and kiss him on the corner of his mouth.

Bram was burningly conscious of her body pressed against his, of the touch of her lips, but he mistrusted the brittleness of her smile, and when he saw her glance at Nick his suspicion deepened.

He saw the other man raise his eyebrows and smile at Sophie in a quick appreciative gesture. What was going on?

There was a tiny silence.

Melissa broke it first. 'Let's see this ring Bram's been telling me about, Sophie,' she said, and Sophie held out her hand, grateful for the change of subject.

Her sister oohed and aahed suitably over the ring. 'It's absolutely lovely, and just right for you—unconventional and warm and colourful.' She smiled warmly at Bram. 'You know Sophie very well!'

Bram thought of the look Sophie had just exchanged with Nick. 'Sometimes I wonder if I do,' he said.

'Come and look at Sophie's ring, Mum,' said Melissa as Harriet came back into the room, followed by Joe, who was carrying a bottle of champagne.

'Very nice,' Harriet approved.

Nick made a big deal of taking Sophie's hand and inspecting the ring closely. Sophie felt one of his fingers caress her palm surreptitiously, and she snatched her hand back, her colour heightened.

'Unusual,' he said.

'Sophie's an unusual person,' said Bram, who hadn't missed Sophie's quick flush.

'Indeed.' Nick seemed amused. 'Still, are you sure you wouldn't have preferred diamonds?' he asked Sophie. 'That's what a real engagement ring should be, after all.'

'No,' said Sophie, meeting his eyes, unspoken challenge in her own. She knew that he was referring to the ring that he had bought for her. That might have been a 'real' engagement, but it hadn't brought her happiness.

'I like rubies best,' she said, and took Bram's hand to underline her point.

'Must have set you back a bit, Bram,' commented Joe, taking his turn to inspect the ring with a grunt. 'I reckon that would have paid for a heifer or two! I hope you thanked him nicely, Sophie?' he teased, the way he had when she and Melissa were little girls.

'I did, but I don't mind saying it again,' said Sophie, not averse to the chance to show Nick just how in love she and Bram were. 'Come under the mistletoe, Bram.'

Tugging him under the dangling mistletoe, she reached up to pull his head gently down to hers. 'Thank you, Bram,' she whispered, her palm warm against his cheek so that she could trace his lip with her thumb and look deep into his eyes.

And then a funny thing happened. She forgot that Nick was watching, forgot to care what he might be thinking. She forgot Melissa and her parents, and the fact that the champagne was getting warm.

She saw only the blueness of Bram's eyes, felt only the urge to press her mouth to his and give herself up to the dizzy, delicious pleasure of kissing him deep and long and slow, and feeling him kiss her back. She wanted the kiss to go on for ever, wanted to sink down with him somewhere soft so that she could pull off that stupid tie, unbutton his shirt and feel his hands ease down the zip of dress...

Heart thudding with excitement at the very thought of it, Sophie gave something between a gasp and a murmur and clutched at him, as if desperate to anchor herself to his solidity, but Bram was already raising his head to break the kiss. For a long moment they just stared at each other, Sophie's expression dazed, Bram's completely unreadable.

Senses still reeling, shaken at the effort it had taken to break away before he lost control, Bram tore his eyes away from hers. Looking around for something, anything, to fix on instead, he saw Joe looking dourly pleased, Harriet indulgent, and Melissa delighted.

Bram's gaze moved on to Nick. The other man's face was perfectly straight, but Bram could swear that he was smirking. He watched as Nick lifted his brows at Sophie with a glance that was a complex mixture of amusement and indulgence. Why not hang out a sign saying that he knew she had kissed Bram merely to prove a point to him? Bram wondered savagely.

Was that why she had done it? He looked at Sophie just in time to see her catch Nick's eye. Colouring, she let her gaze slide away.

So it was. Disappointment twisted like a knife inside Bram. Well, what had he expected? Just because he had fallen in love with her it didn't mean that Sophie felt any differently about Nick. He had been hoping against hope that things would change when she saw him again, but it looked as if she was as closely bound to the other man as ever. He had let himself forget the deal they had made to accept each other as second best.

But how could he remember when Sophie kissed him like that? When he could still feel the warm softness of her body pressed against his, the sweetness of her lips? It was all too easy to let himself believe then that she felt the same sense of rightness in his arms. It wasn't Sophie's fault that being second best wasn't good enough for him now.

Harriet was bustling around, making sure that everyone had a glass of champagne before Joe made a toast to the happy couple.

Still pulsing from that kiss, Sophie hardly heard what

her father was saying. She fixed on a bright smile, but her whole body was throbbing and tingling, and her lips burned. She felt as if she were radiating heat and awareness. They could put her on top of a police car and save on the flashing lights.

To Sophie, emerging from the warmth and sweetness and excitement of kissing Bram, Nick's look had been like a slap in the face. Until then she had forgotten that she had just seized on a chance to prove to him that he was wrong, and remembering made her feel cheap and ashamed of herself.

It hadn't even convinced Nick. That had been obvious. He had made it plain that he realised that she was only kissing Bram to make a point to him, and that the fact amused him.

It wasn't *like* that! Sophie wanted to shout, thinking about that wonderful kiss.

She supposed she must have smiled and said the right thing, because nobody else seemed to notice anything amiss. They all seemed perfectly normal.

Or perhaps not all.

Sophie revised her opinion as they sat down to dinner. Her parents were certainly behaving as usual. Her father was gruffly affectionate, her mother beaming at the success of her family party, but there was a distinct tension in the middle of the table.

Bram was talking pleasantly to her mother and Melissa, but there was a grim look around his mouth and a bleakness to his expression that Sophie hated to see. His shoulders were rigidly set, and when she rested her hand against the small of his back, in an attempt to offer wordless reassurance, it was like touching iron. He was smiling and talking as normal, but she sensed a new distance in him.

Hadn't he wanted her to kiss him? Sophie wondered, dismayed thoughts tumbling around in her head. Surely he must have known that a kiss would be likely at some point? Or was he simply finding it harder than he had thought to be close to Melissa again?

Melissa herself seemed to be blossoming under his attention. Sophie hadn't had a chance to talk to her sister properly yet, but she sensed a tension in her too. She was as lovely as ever, but when Sophie looked more closely she noticed a look of strain around the beautiful violet eyes. Something was wrong, that was for sure. Her mother had described Melissa and Nick as being all over each other normally, but they were barely touching, barely even looking at each other tonight.

Nick, lounging easily across the table from Sophie, ignored his beautiful wife. He was deriving more amusement from playing with Sophie instead. His eyes wandered over her in naked appreciation as he paid her extravagant compliments and needled her about her engagement.

He thinks I'm still in love with him, Sophie realised. He thinks I wore this dress for him.

She hadn't dressed with Nick in mind at all…or had she? With characteristic honesty Sophie asked herself whether she might have subconsciously wanted to make Nick regret losing her. She didn't *think* that she had, but she had thought herself in love with him for so long that it was possible, and she felt humiliated at the thought.

Once she would have glowed at having his exclusive attention, but now it was making her uncomfortable, and she kept trying to draw the others into the conversation.

'I hear you've been on holiday?' she said desperately at last, leaning across the table to Melissa. 'Where did you go?'

'Just Morocco.' Nick answered for his wife, with all the casualness of the seasoned intercontinental traveller. 'We were trekking in the High Atlas.'

'That doesn't sound like you, Melissa,' said Sophie, persevering with her attempt to talk to her sister. 'You were always a beach girl.'

Melissa's answering smile was a little strained. 'I have to admit that I would have preferred to spend the time in a resort, but you know Nick and his mountains...!' she said, trying to make a joke out of it.

Actually, Sophie did know. Nick had told her at length about all his mountaineering exploits, as well as everything else he had done. Nick didn't just climb mountains—oh, no! True, he had climbed peaks in the Andes and the Himalayas and the Alps, but he had also been on expedition in the Amazon, done white water rafting in the Rockies and surveyed rhinos in Africa. He had sailed around Cape Horn and canoed in Polynesia. He had been everywhere and done everything. No wonder she had been bowled over when he had condescended to notice her.

Now she wished she hadn't been so impressed.

'It's much better for you to have an active holiday,' Nick told his wife. 'It's boring sitting on a beach all day.'

For him, maybe, but not for Melissa. For the first time Sophie realised that her sister's marriage might not be as perfect as she had imagined. She had so wanted to marry Nick in Melissa's place—but would she really have wanted him making all the decisions about where they went on holiday and what they did?

Nick's interruptions were beginning to irritate her, too. 'So, how was the trekking?' she asked, pointedly addressing her sister.

'Oh, it was…fine. Great. There were some nice people in the group.'

'Sheep,' said Nick dismissively.

'Just like being out on the moors, then,' said Bram dryly, and Melissa giggled. But Nick quite missed the humour.

'I meant that the people were like sheep,' he explained. 'They just did whatever they were told.'

'I expect that's why they paid to go on a guided tour,' said Sophie. 'Sometimes you don't want to have to work everything out for yourself. Especially when you're in a foreign country.'

Nick was unimpressed. 'The whole trip was a shambles,' he said. 'I've always been an independent traveller, but I'd been so busy with the company that I didn't have time to plan our own route, so I thought we'd see how the other half lives and go on an organised trip. Never again!'

'Why? What happened?'

Nick made a gesture indicating that he didn't know where to start. 'The tour guide didn't seem to have a clue what he was doing—he had no leadership abilities at all!—and it was clear that the local guides were running rings round him. I soon put them right. If I hadn't been there we'd have been ripped off left, right and centre!'

To hear Nick tell it, he had single-handedly rescued the group from the disaster of sticking to the itinerary they had booked and paid for. He had changed the route of a trek that had unaccountably been considered perfectly satisfactory by previous trekkers, and, thanks to his fluency in Arabic, had negotiated a deal for food by coming to separate arrangements with locals whenever they stopped, thus cutting out the local guides, whose contacts had provided sustenance previously.

'Tourists are too easily intimidated,' he said.

'How did the others in the group react to all this?' asked Bram.

'Nobody said anything.' Nick shook his head in wonder at their ingratitude. 'I even gave them copies of our catalogue and the address of our website, *and* we said that we would give them a small discount, and no one has been in touch!'

Sophie glanced at Melissa and saw that she was staring down at her plate, looking distinctly uncomfortable. As Sophie watched, she lifted her lashes and sent Bram a look of naked appeal. Bram smiled and winked at her, and Melissa coloured slightly.

There was something intimate about the tiny exchange, and Sophie wished she hadn't seen it.

Nick was still going on about their trip. 'It was an interesting experiment, but it reminded me how frustrating it is to be in a group. It takes for ever to get everyone ready, and then when you do get going you're always having to slow down to wait for the others to catch up. The only way to really experience things is to go on your own.'

He glanced smugly round the table. 'But then I've always been a maverick that way.'

'I've always understood that you shouldn't walk or climb on your own for safety reasons,' said Bram evenly.

Nick waved his objection aside. 'That's for people who don't know what they're doing,' he said. 'I quite agree that tourists who amble around the moors here need to walk in pairs at least, but I prefer to walk on my own—especially when I'm testing the clothes we sell. When you're experienced you can take things onto a whole new level, without being shackled by a slower pace or intrusive chatter.'

'You're not afraid of getting lost?' said Bram, wondering what it was about Nick that Melissa and Sophie could possibly love so much. 'The moors can be quite deceptive.'

'Not when you know what you're doing.' Nick helped himself to more wine and sat back, ready to illuminate them. 'It's a matter of instinct. I've been out in the wilds enough to know how to get myself out of trouble, no matter what happens.'

'I hope you do.' Bram kept his voice even. 'I get called out by Mountain Rescue several times every winter, and it would be embarrassing if it turned out to be for a member of the family.'

Nick laughed heartily. 'That's not going to happen! The thing is, *you* just know one tiny section of the moors where you farm,' he told Bram, with a patronising smile. 'It's natural you should be cautious about venturing beyond that. When you have wider experience to draw on, as I do, you feel confident anywhere, no matter what the conditions.'

He launched into a lengthy account of all the times when his mastery of survival techniques had enabled him to triumph over the odds in the wilder parts of the world. To hear his talk of battling against the elements, one would never believe that he lived in a comfortable detached house in Pickering.

Bram switched off after a while. It was hard to concentrate anyway when Sophie was sitting beside him in that dress. She looked so lush and gorgeous his hands itched to reach out and touch her. She had finished eating and was studying her glass, her eyes lowered so that it was impossible to know what she was thinking.

Was she as bored and irritated as he was? Or was she loving the sound of Nick's voice? Was she impressed by his stories and wishing that she could be with him? Was she wishing that it was Nick she had kissed earlier?

The kiss, that sweet kiss, had been designed as a message for Nick, Bram knew. It had had nothing to do with him, he realised bitterly, withdrawing behind a barrier of hurt pride. It had been a message for him too. Sophie might be wearing his ring, but it was Nick that she was thinking about, Nick she still wanted.

Well, she had never pretended otherwise, had she? And Nick was still married to Melissa. Perhaps he could accept being second best, Bram thought, if he were married to Sophie. Something was better than nothing. He would see her every day, and be with her, and if he was patient she might come to love him the way he so suddenly and so desperately loved her.

Until then, Bram decided, he would have to settle for being friends.

Sophie didn't get a chance to talk to her sister alone until just before they were ready to leave. She met Melissa on the landing, on her way back from the bathroom, and the two sisters hugged. 'It's been lovely to see you again, Mel,' Sophie told her in a rush of affection. 'I'm sorry it's been so long.'

Melissa clung to her. 'I'm sorry too,' she said. 'I've missed you.'

Her voice cracked and Sophie held her sister away from her and looked into her face in concern. 'Mel, is everything OK?'

'Of course.' Melissa dabbed her eyes in embarrassment. 'I was just getting all emotional.' She managed a wobbly smile. 'You know what I'm like!'

Sophie frowned, unconvinced. 'Are things all right with Nick?'

'Oh, yes. Well, he's sometimes a bit… But, yes, everything's fine,' said Melissa, and rushed on before Sophie had a chance to enquire any closer. 'This is your evening, Sophie. I haven't had a chance to tell you properly how happy I am for you. Bram's such a star. I think he's wonderful—so kind and understanding…'

She sounded on the verge of tears again.

'Hey,' said Sophie, hoping to lighten the atmosphere. 'You've had your chance with Bram! I hope you're not changing your mind? He's mine now,' she joked.

'Of course not.' Melissa's laugh sounded a little forced to Sophie. 'I just hope you know how lucky you are to have a man like Bram. He's really special.'

Sophie thought about Bram, about his steadiness and his strength and the directness of his eyes. She thought about how safe it felt to lean against him, how good it felt to kiss him, and a strange feeling uncurled deep inside her.

'Yes,' she said. 'I know.'

'Thank goodness *that's* over,' said Sophie with a sigh as they drove back to Haw Gill.

As always, the farewells had seemed to take for ever. She longed to ask what Bram had said to Melissa as he hugged her goodbye. Sophie thought that he had held her sister for longer than was strictly necessary, but Melissa hadn't objected. She had smiled and nodded, but then Sophie's mother had claimed her attention, to discuss last-minute wedding details, and she hadn't seen any more.

Now she studied Bram from under her lashes as he drove along the dark moorland lanes. In the muted light from the dashboard he looked withdrawn, almost stern.

'Was...was it awful for you?' she asked hesitantly, not sure that she really wanted to hear that he was still in love with Melissa but feeling that she ought to acknowledge how difficult it must have been for him.

Something had happened during the evening, that much she knew. Bram hadn't carried her back to the car, the way he had when they arrived, and when Sophie thought about the mud on her lovely shoes she wanted to cry. There seemed something symbolic about it somehow.

'It certainly wasn't the best night of my life.' Bram answered her question at last. He glanced at her and then returned his gaze to the road ahead. 'Nick hardly took his eyes off you all evening.'

Sophie felt herself flush in the darkness. 'I think Nick may be the kind of man who's more interested if you're not available than if you are,' she admitted painfully, staring straight ahead.

'Is that why you were at such pains to make it look as if you were in love with me?'

The hardness in Bram's voice made her head jerk round. 'What do you mean?'

'That's why you kissed me like that, isn't it?' said Bram. 'You wanted to make him think that you weren't interested in him any more.'

Fatally, Sophie hesitated. She *had* wanted Nick to think that, she remembered, ashamed. 'Yes,' she said, unwilling to lie to Bram. 'Partly, anyway. But—'

'You don't need to explain, Sophie,' he interrupted her. 'I understand.'

'But—' she began helplessly, not even sure what she

was going to say. But Bram wasn't going to listen anyway.

'I don't think we should talk about it,' he said. 'We both know what the situation is, and nothing has changed for either of us.'

It's changed for me, she wanted to say. But she didn't know how or why.

She just knew that it had.

CHAPTER NINE

BRAM came into the kitchen, rubbing his hands against the cold. 'I don't like the look of that sky,' he said. 'I'm going to bring the last of the sheep in off the moor, so I might not be back for lunch until later.'

Sophie was at the table, spooning mincemeat into pastry cases for mince pies. Outside the window, the moors looked bleaker than usual, frozen white and solid under clouds which hung so low they blurred the horizon. They bulged with the ominous yellow greyness that signalled snow, and probably lots of it.

She frowned and brushed flour from her apron. Snow wasn't unusual up here on the moors, but it was easy to get caught out. 'Do you want a hand?' she asked.

'Bess and I will manage.'

Sophie bit her lip. Nothing had been the same since the dinner to celebrate their engagement. It was nearly two weeks since that tense evening, but it seemed like longer.

Bram had refused to discuss that evening, Nick or Melissa any further. The next morning he'd been his usual calm, friendly self, and ostensibly they had gone back to the way they were before. But Sophie sensed a greater distance in him now, as if there was something tightly leashed inside him, and she didn't know what had caused it or what she could do to make it better.

While she worried about it, the arrangements for the wedding rolled inexorably on. Her wedding dress was hanging up at Glebe Farm, the caterers had been organised down to the last parsley garnish, and the flowers were being delivered first thing on Christmas Eve.

'But I can't find a hairdresser or anyone to do your make-up who's free to come out on Christmas Eve,' her mother had lamented. 'You'll have to do the best you can. You will make an effort to look nice, won't you?'

'Of course,' Sophie had said, but the wedding seemed like something vague and unreal that her mother talked about. It was hard for her to believe in it herself when she was preoccupied with Bram.

She couldn't seem to talk to him at the moment. When she tried, he would change the conversation, pleasantly but firmly, and retreat behind a barrier of horribly polite friendliness. Sophie was terribly afraid that he was seriously regretting his offer of marriage as a way out of her problems.

It made her realise for the first time how much she did want to marry him. She would miss him, miss Haw Gill and their isolated life up on the moors. Leaving now would be doubly hard, but she couldn't stay if it was going to make Bram unhappy. She couldn't bear that.

And sooner or later they were going to have to talk about it. It was the twentieth of December already. In a few days' time it would be too late. Sophie had been rehearsing how she might raise the issue as she made the mince pies, but she wasn't sorry to be diverted now Bram had come in, and the prospect of snow offered a welcome distraction.

There was no point in trying to talk while Bram was thinking about the sheep up on the moor, but tonight, Sophie vowed, tonight she would make him listen.

'At least have some coffee before you go,' she said, moving over to set the kettle on the range. 'I'll make you a sandwich too. You shouldn't go up there without something to eat.'

'OK. Thanks,' said Bram, anxious to get on his way but knowing that what she suggested was sensible.

He warmed his hands by the wood-burning stove and watched Sophie as she moved around the kitchen. She was wearing his mother's old apron, and there was a smudge of flour on her cheek where she had brushed her hair away from her face as she was rolling out the pastry.

He wished that they had never gone to that engagement dinner. He had been hoping against hope that when Sophie came face to face with Nick again she would find that the magic had gone, but it had been clear instead that there was still something between them. Nick had had his interest piqued; that was obvious, and as for Sophie—why would she be so determined to show Nick that she was over him unless she still cared desperately about what he thought?

That kiss, that piercingly sweet kiss, had been for Nick's benefit, not Bram's. Sophie had admitted it herself. Bram told himself that it was unfair to resent her when she had never tried to hide how she felt for Nick. He knew that he was one who had suggested himself as second best. It hadn't been her idea. He just hadn't bargained for how much it would hurt him.

The only way he could deal with it was to seal himself off as much as he could. He could see that Sophie sensed that something was wrong, and wanted to talk about it, but what could he say other than that he loved her and that he didn't want to be second best, after all? That wasn't the deal they had made, and all Bram could do was to try and stick to that as far as he could.

Sophie put a mug of coffee and a hearty ham sandwich in front of him and looked worriedly at the tiny flakes drifting down outside the window. 'It's starting to snow.'

'I'll get going as soon as I've had this.' Bram kept an eye on the snow as he drank the coffee gratefully. It was hot and strong—just what he needed. The snow was barely more than spitting at the moment. Certainly nothing to get too worried about yet.

'I wonder if we'll have a white Christmas this year,' said Sophie, sitting down opposite him and cupping her hands around her own mug of coffee.

'Might do,' said Bram, his mouth full of sandwich. 'It's cold enough out there, and if it does snow heavily it'll lie. The ground's like iron.'

'I thought I'd get out Molly's decorations this afternoon,' she said hesitantly. 'She always made the sitting room look so pretty at Christmas. I'd like to do it for her.'

He smiled at her, Nick and his own uncertainties forgotten for the moment. 'She would have liked that. Shall I find a tree in the wood?'

'Oh, that would be wonderful.' Sophie's face lit up. She had been wondering how to ask him, afraid that the loss of his mother would make it too painful for him.

'I think it'll be too late by the time I get back this afternoon, but we'll go and look tomorrow,' Bram promised.

Sophie's smile faded as he drained his mug of coffee and began putting on layers of jumpers and jackets. 'How long do you think you'll be?'

'It depends where the sheep are.' Bram's voice was muffled as he pulled a fleece over his head. 'If they're waiting by the gate to be fed there shouldn't be a problem, but if they're sheltering under one of other walls it might take a bit of time to find them.'

To Sophie's anxious eye, the snow was already thickening. 'You be careful,' she said, hugging him, and Bram's arms, much padded by that stage, came round her and held her tight for a moment.

'Don't worry about me,' he said. 'I've got Bess to look after me.' Awkward in all his layers, he moved to the kitchen door to put on his boots. 'I'll be back as soon as I can.'

And then he was gone. Sophie finished her mince pies and put them to bake in the range, all the time watching the snow outside the window. It seemed to be falling faster by the second. What had once been fine flecks were now thick flakes of snow, spiralling steadily downwards and settling on the stiff branches of the trees and Molly's pots of herbs just outside the kitchen door.

Sophie couldn't settle. The sky grew darker and the snow fell more heavily, blanketing the moors in white until it was impossible to tell the ground from the sky. If only Bram would come in she might enjoy it.

She had checked the fridge and the freezer. They had plenty of food to see them through, and more than enough firewood stored. If it carried on snowing they might even be snowed in for a while. Haw Gill Farm was at the end of the track, and it wasn't unusual for it to be cut off for several days. Sophie could think of worse things than to be shut in a warm farmhouse with Bram. They could have Christmas on their own and everyone else could have the wedding without them.

Outside, it was bitterly cold, and the snow was swirling with a new intensity as a fierce wind picked up momentum over the moors and hurtled towards the farmhouse. It was frightening how quickly conditions could change. Sophie tried to push the word 'blizzard' from her mind, and concentrated on how far Bram might have got instead. If only mobile phones worked up here. She could at least ring him then, and find out where he was. As it was, she just had to wait.

Tomorrow would be the shortest day. There was little enough light as it was, even without the snow, and by half past three it was too dark to see beyond the white flakes swirling at the window. Sophie paced restlessly back and forwards to the kitchen door. Every now and then she would stand in the open doorway, wiping the snow flurries from her face, and strain her ears for the sound of Bram and the dog over the howling wind.

Bram knew what he was doing. There was no need to panic, Sophie told herself endlessly. But she was very close to panic nonetheless by the time the sound of the door opening had her bolting from her restless perch by the fire. She practically ran across the room and wrenched open the door to the utility room, where Bram stood, barely recognisable beneath his riming of snow, attempting to towel the worst of the snow off poor Bess.

'Thank God you're back!' Sophie threw her arms round him, dislodging a shower of snow, and hugged him tightly. Bram managed a tired grin, but he didn't hug her back. He might have been too cold and bundled up to move easily, or perhaps he was embarrassed by her welcome.

Afraid that it might be the latter, Sophie took the towel from him and bent to deal with the dog so that he could strip off his outside layers. 'I was beginning to think you were lost up there,' she said, not looking at him.

'I nearly was. The sheep had taken themselves right over the far side of the moor, and by the time we found them it was snowing so hard we had a hard time making it back. But Bess did a grand job.' Bram bent to pat the dog, who thumped her tail wearily.

'It's too cold for you in your kennel,' Sophie told her. 'You'd better come in by the fire.'

So Bess was allowed to stretch blissfully in front of the wood-burning stove, a position she had long coveted, while Sophie made Bram some tea and fussed around him, taking away his cold, wet outer clothes until he sat in his shirt and trousers, his feet in thick grey socks stretched out towards the fire.

He sighed contentedly as he took a sip of the hot tea. 'I dreamed of this up on the moor,' he said. 'A lot of the time I could hardly see where I was going, but I kept thinking of getting back to this kitchen and being able to sit in front of the fire like this. I imagined it being warm and full of good smells, like it is.'

He paused, glancing at Sophie, who was draping his fleece over the drying rack that hung above the range. 'And I thought about you being here,' he said.

Sophie's hands stilled at the note in his voice, and she looked over her shoulder to meet his blue, blue eyes. 'It made a difference to know that you would be here, waiting for me,' he said.

His words set a warmth uncoiling deep inside her, spreading outwards until she was flooded with it. Unable to tear her gaze away, Sophie could only look back at him and feel the heat tingling under her skin. 'I'm glad I was here, too,' she said.

The tension that had been so much part of the atmosphere for the last few weeks was melting like the last few snowflakes on Bess's coat. Sophie let out a long breath, one that she hadn't been aware that she was holding. Thank goodness, she thought. Now we'll be able to talk.

It was at that moment that the phone rang, its insistent buzzing startling them both. 'If this is my mother about flower arrangements...!' said Sophie vengefully as she went to pick it up.

But it wasn't her mother. It was Melissa, sounding on the verge of hysteria. 'Nick's missing,' she burst out, before Sophie had finished saying hello. 'He set off to walk on the moors this afternoon, and he said he'd be back before dark.'

'He went for a *walk*?' said Sophie incredulously. Outside the wind was howling over the moors, smashing snow against the window. 'In this?'

'He wanted to test out some new cold weather trousers that we're stocking,' said Melissa. 'He said he was just going to walk up Pike Fell, then over the moor to you, and back down the road. It's a perfectly straightforward route.'

'Not in a blizzard,' said Sophie.

'He's well prepared,' Melissa said defensively. 'He knows what he's doing. He's not a fool.'

Sophie didn't bother to answer that. 'Have you called Mountain Rescue?'

'No! Nick would kill me. Think what it would do to his reputation!'

'Melissa, he might be hurt. We've got to find him!'

'He won't have wandered off the route,' said Melissa stubbornly. 'We don't need to call in anyone else. Dad's just got back from checking this side of the fell. If you could just ask Bram to walk your bit of the moors, I'm sure he'd find him. He might just have slipped and not be able to walk very fast.'

Or he might be unconscious, or lost and disorientated in the blizzard. Sophie looked helplessly at Bram. He was exhausted. The last thing he needed was to set off into the snow again—but what choice did they have? It was too cold to risk Nick spending the night in the open.

Bram had been listening to Sophie's half of the conversation, and from her expression it wasn't hard to put together what had happened. Getting up, he took the phone from Sophie.

'Melissa, tell me when Nick set off…where was he heading?' He listened briefly. 'OK, now call Mountain Rescue and tell them what you told me. If you don't, I will. Tell them I'm setting off towards Pike Fell. I'll take one possible route up to the top, and another down, and I'll check in when I get back.' His voice softened. 'Don't worry, Mel. I'll find him for you.'

Sophie's face was white, and Bram read her fear for Nick in her eyes as he put down the phone. He took hold of her shoulders. 'I won't bother telling you not to worry, but there's no need to panic. Melissa says that Nick's got all the right equipment with him.'

Sophie was more afraid for him than for Nick right then, but she knew there was no point in trying to stop him going. 'I'm going to put on some warmer clothes,' she said.

Bram frowned. 'You don't need to come.'

'I do,' said Sophie. 'I'm not having two of you out there on your own. You're already tired. That's when accidents happen. You know it makes sense for there to be two of us. And I want to do what I can too.'

She was half afraid that he would have set out without her by the time she came down, pulling a second jumper over her head, but he had found some dry clothes to change into and was testing two flashlights. He gave one to Sophie when she had struggled into an oilskin coat and trousers and was bundled up in hat and scarf and gloves so that only her eyes were visible. Then he slung a rucksack with emergency supplies and a first aid kit over his shoulder.

'Stay together for now,' he shouted in her ear as they set off, Bess at his heel as usual.

Sophie nodded, unable to speak. The wind snatched her breath away and the snow hurled itself at her, no longer the soft, beautifully drifting flakes she had admired earlier, but driving, icy needles that stung her from every direction. Keeping her head down, she trudged after Bram.

The snow was already drifting where there was the slightest resistance against the wind, and when they reached the gate leading into the first field it was already difficult to push it open. Yelling into her ear over the scream of the wind, Bram told her to work her way round the edge of the field. 'Stick to the wall the whole way,' he shouted. 'Even if it's harder walking. If you lose it, you'll get disorientated. We'll meet up at the next gate.'

Sophie struggled up through the snowy heather, swinging her torch from side to side and shouting Nick's name—although it was impossible that anyone could hear anything through the howling wind and the blinding snow. How would they ever be able to find him in this?

It had been OK with Bram's solid figure just in front of her, but now she began to feel frightened. The wind was just too strong, the snow too driving. Her face and her hands were numb with cold and the lack of visibility was disorientating. She couldn't tell where she was, or how far she had to go.

The wall seemed endless, but at last it turned and led her towards the gate, where the glimpse of Bram's flash-light was the best thing Sophie had ever seen. He loomed suddenly out of the swirling snow, and they both shook their heads.

They set off separately again. Sophie walked bent forwards against the wind, which bullied and pushed her around mercilessly, driving snow into her numb face. Sometimes she fell over a clump of heather and it was hard to get upright again. *Stick to the wall, stick to the wall,* she chanted inside her head. It would be too easy to lose it in these conditions. She moved close enough to be able to touch the stones for reassurance if she needed to, and that was how she came across the steps, which were little more than flat stones built into the wall so that walkers could climb over easily.

Sophie knocked her knee against one and fell over. She was struggling to her feet once more when she remembered that they led to a gully which offered a shortcut back down to the road. It meant a bit of a scramble over the rocks, but in summer it saved a couple of miles' hard walking across the heather. In winter, though, and in these conditions, it would be a treacherous route.

Surely Nick wouldn't have gone that way today?

Sophie hesitated about leaving the safety of the wall, but the impulse to check was so strong that eventually she climbed over the wall and promptly plunged into a deep drift the other side. Sodden and shivering, she struggled to the edge of the gully, which was so well disguised in the snow that she nearly fell over it herself.

Flashing her torch, she saw a faint answering flash from the bottom. Should she go and find Bram? Or get down to look for Nick? Trusting that when she didn't turn up at the gate Bram would come and find her, Sophie floundered back to the steps and somehow managed to wedge her scarf under a rock, where it flapped frantically. Surely Bram would see it and realise where she had gone?

Very carefully, she picked her way down to bottom of the gully. There she found Nick, enveloped in an orange survival bag and already half covered by insulating snow. 'I fell,' he managed to tell her through lips that were stiff with cold. 'I've done something to my knee. I couldn't get back up the slope, so I thought I should insulate myself as far as I could and wait for daylight. I've got emergency supplies,' he explained, seeing Sophie's face. 'I know how to survive. I'd have been fine.'

But what about her and Bram, struggling through a night like this in search of him? After the first rush of relief at finding him alive, Sophie was furious with him. 'I'll go back and see if I can find Bram,' she said. 'At least we know where you are now.'

She had just made it up to the top of the gully once more when a black shape almost knocked her over. It was Bess, barking to alert Bram, who appeared seconds later. Sophie sagged with relief at the sight of him, but it was Bram's turn to be furious. He grabbed her by the shoulders and brought his face close to hers so that he could shout at her.

'What the hell do you think you're doing? I told you to stick to the wall!'

'Nick…' was all Sophie could stutter, so cold and so tired that she could hardly speak at all. 'He's in the gully!'

Bram swore. 'I don't care where he is! You shouldn't have left the wall. You're a bloody fool! You could have fallen and hurt yourself, and then how would I have found you?'

'I left you my scarf as a sign by the steps. You must have seen it.'

'There's no scarf now. I only came this way because Bess was insistent. She kept barking and jumping onto the wall.'

'Oh, Bess!' Close to tears, Sophie bent to pat her shakily. 'You're a rescue dog.'

Bram was struggling to contain his fury, which had been fuelled by the cold fear of Sophie lost and alone in the blizzard. 'We'd better get down to Nick,' he said after a moment, deciding not to give her any more grief until they were both warm and dry again. 'Show me where he is.'

Afterwards, Sophie couldn't remember how they got Nick back to the farmhouse. There was just the numbness in her hands and her feet, the freezing snow, and the relentless, horrifying scream of the wind as they battled over the heather, supporting Nick between them. Without her scarf, there was nothing to protect her neck from the onslaught of snow. It drove into the slightest gap, numbing her skin and trickling inside her jacket, seeping through her jumpers until she was chilled to the bone. The only thing that kept her going was Bram, walking steadily onwards, bearing most of Nick's weight, constantly encouraging them both and refusing to let them give up and sink down into the snow to rest.

'Not much further,' he kept saying. 'You can do it.'

Sophie felt as if she were trapped in some terrible nightmare, but Bram was right. They did do it, and at last the lights of Haw Gill glowed through the blur of snow. Inside, Bram took charge. He let Nick and Sophie sit, dull with exhaustion, in front of the fire, while he rang Melissa and called off the search.

'The road's blocked,' he said when he'd put the phone

down. 'It looks as if you'll be staying here a couple of days, Nick. I don't think there's much that can be done about your knee anyway, other than to rest it.'

Nick's bravado had deserted him after that terrible journey back to the house, and he was too tired to object when Bram helped him upstairs and made him take off his wet clothes.

'Put him in my bed,' said Sophie, forcing herself to her feet. 'It's warmer in there. I'll bring up a hot water bottle.'

'Take off your own clothes first,' said Bram roughly, concerned at the flat marks of exhaustion on her face.

'Why, Bram,' she said, trying to lighten the atmosphere with a joke, 'is this any time for you to be making a suggestion like that? I've got to say that your seduction technique needs work!'

A tired smile flickered over his face as he hauled Nick up from his chair. 'I'll have to try harder,' he agreed, and as their eyes met over Nick's slumped head there was a moment, just a moment, when Sophie could have sworn that there was a sizzle in the air.

The thought of it kept her warm as, shivering, she stripped off her sodden clothes and clambered into blissfully dry pyjamas, and it made her pause as she belted one of Molly's old dressing gowns around her. She had never cared what she looked like before, but now, for the first time, she wondered what it would be like to go down to meet Bram in a seductive nightdress, to wrap herself in silk that would slither off her shoulders at the slightest touch of his hands...

The image stayed with her as they shared a pot of hot, sweet tea and made a fuss of Bess, whose heroism had already been amply rewarded to her dog's mind by her being fed and allowed a place in front of the fire.

Exhausted by her endeavours, she lay snoring and twitching slightly, utterly oblivious to Sophie's simmering awareness of Bram.

Bram seemed oblivious too. He looked very tired, and they didn't talk much, but he made Sophie eat something, and she put the persistent shivery feeling under her skin down to exhaustion, cold, and emotional overload.

'Come on,' said Bram, seeing her yawn. 'It's time you were in bed.'

'I think I'm too tired to move,' Sophie confessed.

'I'll help you.' Reaching down a hand, he lifted her to her feet and kept hold of her as they climbed the stairs together, his grip warm and strong and indescribably comforting.

Halfway up, Sophie remembered that Nick was sound asleep in her bed. 'I'd better make up a bed,' she said wearily, but she was swaying with tiredness and Bram simply steered her into his room.

'Neither of us is in any state to start fussing about sheets,' he said. 'Why don't you sleep with me tonight? I promise you I'm too tired to take advantage of you,' he added, with a ghost of a smile.

'I'm too tired to notice if you did,' said Sophie frankly, glad that he had taken the decision out of her hands. She was certainly too tired to feel anything except relief as she tumbled into bed beside Bram. 'God, what a day!'

The sheets were cold, and she shivered and kicked her feet to warm them. 'I should have got us a hot water bottle.'

'Come here,' said Bram, lifting his arm, and after a moment she snuggled into his body, feeling his arm close around her. It should have been awkward to be lying so intimately together, but the warmth of his body was incredibly reassuring. With a sigh of comfort, Sophie rested her own arm across his, feeling the slow, steady rise and fall of his chest, and fell at once into a deep and fathomless sleep.

Bram woke early, as usual. Sophie was sleeping softly against him, and he lay for a while, treasuring the feel of her warm, relaxed body so close to his. The wind had dropped some time in the night, but the muffled quality to the light when it eventually seeped through the curtains told him that the snow was very deep.

'Talk about deep and crisp and even,' said Sophie later, when they went out to find a Christmas tree as promised.

Bram had been out feeding the stock when she woke up, and she had made herself some tea before taking a mug to Nick. To her dismay, he had been far from embarrassed about the trouble he had caused, and looked on the previous day's events as further proof of his ability to survive in dangerous conditions.

'Of course most people would have just given up if they'd found themselves in my position,' he had said complacently. 'But I knew exactly what I needed to do.'

Most people would have known better than to set off at all, Sophie had thought, but she'd kept her thoughts to herself. She'd left him phoning Melissa, and been glad to escape with Bram in search of a tree.

'Anything's better than paperwork,' Bram had said when he'd come back, and had suggested an expedition to the wood that lay in a fold of the hill behind the farmhouse.

They had played there as children, and it had always seemed a magical place to Sophie. Today, with the snow blanketing everything in dazzling white, it was more beautiful than ever. It was very still, and there were only occasional traces of little creatures who had scurried over the snow. In the trees, the birds huddled together and fluffed up their feathers for warmth, watching as Sophie and Bram searched for a suitable tree, their voices ringing in the silence.

At last they found a pine that had put itself in amongst the native trees. It was about six foot high, and a little lopsided, but Sophie voted it perfect.

'If this is the one you want...' Bram began chopping.

Sophie watched his shoulders swinging the axe in a steady movement. She was glad that he hadn't brought the chainsaw, whose whine would have spoilt the still magic of the day. Instead, there was just the slow thud of metal against wood, the sound of her own breathing, and Bram's intent face.

And the sudden, overwhelming realisation that she was in love with him.

How could she not have known it before? Sophie wondered. Of course she had always loved Bram—but not like this; not with this heart-wrenching, aching certainty. She had loved him as a friend for so long that she hadn't noticed when affection had become desire, when liking had tipped into need.

This wasn't the desperate, dramatic love she had felt for Nick. In the very fibre of her being Sophie knew that her love for Bram was deeper, truer, stronger than that. Loving Nick had been a firework that had exploded in her world in dazzling colours, only to fizzle out without trace. She had clung to the memory of how spectacular it had been, but the love itself had gone. Loving Bram was a flame that had glowed steadily deep inside her, growing so slowly that she hadn't even noticed until it burned in every part of her, in every sense and every cell.

It seemed to Sophie that the whole day was suffused with joy as they dragged the tree back over the snow, Bess snuffling happily ahead of them. She wanted to shout it out loud, to spin and stretch out her arms in delight, but memory stopped her—the memory of doing precisely that in front of Bram. She had told him then how much she loved Nick. How feeble would it sound to say now that she had changed her mind?

She had no reason to suppose that Bram had changed *his* mind, Sophie reminded herself. An effusive announcement of how much she loved him after all might simply make him feel awkward if he couldn't return her feelings. But they were going to be married. She felt the engagement ring on her finger and clung to the thought. There would be time to tell him that she loved him.

Time and opportunity. *I'll wait until you're ready,* he had said, when they had talked about sleeping together. *All you've got to do is say.* Surely in the dark, with their arms around each other, their bodies close together, she could tell him the truth?

All she had to do was say. Sophie looked at Bram, outlined in dazzling clarity against the snow, and thrilled at the thought... But how could she when Nick would be there the whole time?

He had got himself downstairs by the time they got back with the tree, so they had lunch together, and afterwards he insisted on watching as Sophie decorated the tree. Sophie didn't want him there. She wanted Bram to help her carefully lift the shining baubles out of the box and hang them on the green branches. She wanted Bram to untangle the string of lights and straighten the trunk and enjoy the tangy fragrance of pine needles.

But when Nick had announced his intention of keeping Sophie company Bram had said that he would spend the afternoon catching up on paperwork, so she was left to decorate the tree with Nick's hot eyes on her. Once, such time alone with him would have been her heart's desire, Sophie thought bitterly. Be careful what you wish for—wasn't that the old saying? How true it was.

It was almost as if Nick was determined to keep her and Bram apart. He monopolised the conversation all evening, quite unchastened by his experience.

Sophie listened with gritted teeth, increasingly embarrassed to think that she had been so in love with him for so long. When she looked back, her relationship with Nick had been very short and very intense. It had only been at the engagement dinner that she had glimpsed the obnoxious side to him. She was strongly tempted to point out how irresponsible he had been now, but she held her tongue for Melissa's sake, afraid that it might escalate into a full-blown row. If she heard about it, her sister would be desperately upset, and Sophie didn't want the atmosphere to be any tenser than it already was for her father's birthday.

She suspected that even Bram's famously calm temper was being strained by Nick's behaviour, but that he too was thinking about Melissa and her parents as he let Nick talk on and accept being waited on hand and foot as his due.

It was a huge relief when Nick finally decided that he was tired and allowed Bram to help him upstairs to bed. At least now they might have some time alone, Sophie thought, hardly able to wait until she had seen that Nick had shut the door to his room. She and Bram could go to bed and snuggle down under the duvet to keep warm together, and surely then she would be able to talk to him at last.

But that was not to be either. Bram turned to her and nodded down the corridor. 'I made up a bed for you in the other room while you were cooking supper. I thought you might be more comfortable in there tonight.'

So that was that. Sophie smiled brightly. 'Great. Thanks.'

They were still getting married, she told herself as she lay cold and lonely in the spare room. The snow would melt, Nick would go, and *then*…then they would be alone and she could tell Bram how she felt.

It was time for the truth.

CHAPTER TEN

THERE was no sign of a thaw the next day. Bram busied himself with jobs in the farm sheds, and Nick decided that he had overdone it the day before and should rest his knee in bed. Sophie had to run up and downstairs, taking him cups of tea and breakfast and little snacks.

'You're an angel,' Nick said as she put a cup of coffee and a couple of biscuits on the bedside table for him. He patted the side of the bed. 'Sit down.'

'I've got some soup on,' Sophie prevaricated, but he wasn't letting her slip away.

'The soup can wait a bit, can't it?' he said plaintively. 'It's very lonely up here on my own!'

So much for the man who travelled fastest alone.

'Come on,' he coaxed as she hesitated still, and he smiled his most devastating smile. 'It's not like you don't know me, is it?'

Unable to think of a reason to refuse immediately, Sophie perched reluctantly on the side of the bed.

'You're nervous of me,' said Nick softly, but she had a feeling that he was secretly pleased. 'You shouldn't be. You know I'd never hurt you.'

But you did, thought Sophie. You hurt me terribly.

Nick's voice deepened. 'I know it's hard for you to keep your feelings under control.'

Sophie looked at him and thought about Bram. 'Yes, it is.'

'That was one of the things I always loved about you,' he went on, as if she hadn't spoken. 'You were so wild and passionate about everything. You seem to have lost that fire, Sophie,' he said regretfully. 'Was it me? Did I do that to you? I couldn't help myself, you know,' he tried to explain. 'Melissa is so beautiful. She's like a dream.'

Was that how Melissa seemed to Bram too? 'I know,' said Sophie dully.

Nick took her hand. 'I still think of you, Sophie. I love Melissa, of course, but she doesn't have your feistiness. When I saw you the other night wearing that dress, and yesterday when you came in from the snow…you looked so alive. You were glowing and your eyes were shining… I couldn't help remembering the good times we had. You think of them too, don't you?'

'You're married to my sister, Nick.' She tried to pull her hand away, but he was holding it too tightly. 'There's no point in remembering them.'

'But you do anyway.' He smiled knowingly. 'This is your room, isn't it? I know you're not sleeping with Bram, and I know that's because you still have feelings for me. It's all right, Sophie, I understand.'

Tugging her hand free at last, Sophie stood up. 'Actually, Nick, I don't think you do,' she said.

'Am I interrupting something?' Bram's voice from the doorway made them both start, and Sophie swung round to see him looking bleaker than she had ever seen him look before.

How long had he been there? Had he seen Nick holding her hand? In spite of herself, she flushed. 'No,' she said as she walked past him. 'Nothing at all.'

'Absolutely nothing,' Nick agreed demurely.

Bram restrained the urge to wipe the complacent smile off the other man's face. 'I just came to ask if you wanted me to help you get downstairs,' he said grittily.

If he found that Nick had been upsetting Sophie by tantalising her with impossible dreams, he would…he would… Well, what could he do? Just be there to help pick up the pieces, as before.

'That's kind,' said Nick, graciously accepting his offer, and apparently determined not to allow Sophie any time alone with Bram. 'It's such a bore losing the use of my knee like this.'

Bram thought of the blizzard, of Sophie's white face and the exhaustion in her eyes. Of the terrible fear when he realised that she had left the wall and that he might not be able to find her.

'Just be glad that's all you lost,' he said grimly.

The sun came out the next day, and with it the snow ploughs. Bram was able to get the tractor out and clear the track down to the road, and he had barely finished before Melissa appeared in a smart four-wheel-drive to take Nick to hospital for a check-up.

'I don't need to go to hospital,' Nick said ungraciously. 'I'm perfectly all right. I just need to rest my knee.'

It took Melissa ages to coax him into the car. When he was finally settled, she came back to say goodbye to Bram and Sophie, who were both trying hard not to show how relieved they felt to see the back of Nick.

Melissa hugged Bram tightly. 'Thank you,' she whispered.

'I said I'd find him for you, didn't I?' said Bram, enfolding her in a comforting embrace.

'You did,' agreed Melissa, smiling through her tears. 'That's the wonderful thing about you, Bram. You always do what you say you're going to do.'

He had said that he would love Melissa for ever, Sophie thought dully. Was he going to do that, too?

It was going to happen all over again. Sophie loved her sister dearly, and she didn't want to resent her. She knew Melissa couldn't help being beautiful. She would never deliberately try to steal any man from Sophie. It wasn't Melissa's fault that the only two men Sophie had ever loved were enthralled by her.

She shouldn't be surprised, Sophie told herself, and she had no right to be hurt. She had always known what Bram felt about Melissa. She had had no trouble accepting it when she'd thought of him as a dear friend, but now that she loved him in a very different way it hurt more than Sophie had thought possible to realise that once again she would have to take second place to her sister.

Still, she raised a smile as Melissa turned to her and hugged her.

'Thank you too, Sophie,' she said. 'Nick says you were an absolute heroine.'

'Not me,' said Sophie. 'Bess was the only heroine that night.'

'Bess hasn't been looking after him since,' Melissa pointed out. 'I'm just so grateful to you both,' she said, including Bram in her glance as she turned for the car. 'See you tonight, then.'

'Tonight?'

'It's Dad's birthday.' Melissa stared at Sophie. 'Surely you haven't forgotten!'

'Oh…no. No…of course not.'

'And you're getting married tomorrow. You do remember that, don't you?' said Melissa, only half joking.

'Of course,' said Sophie with dignity. Although in fact it was easy to lose track of the days when you were cut off by the snow. It was a bit like having jet lag, not being sure of what time it was or where you fitted into the daily routine. 'I'm not likely to forget my own wedding, am I?'

'You never know with you, Sophie,' said Melissa with unaccustomed dryness. 'You're in a world of your own sometimes! Just to warn you, though, Mum's expecting you to sleep at Glebe Farm tonight.'

Sophie looked at her sister in dismay. 'Why?'

'You know what she's like about tradition. There's no question of the bride and groom seeing each other before the wedding, so make sure you bring all your stuff with you when you come tonight. Otherwise there'll just be a scene—and we don't want that on Dad's birthday, do we?'

Sophie was quiet as she got ready that evening. The next day was her wedding day, and she was marrying the man she loved. She should be on top of the world. But it was impossible to relax and enjoy it when she wasn't sure how Bram really felt.

There never seemed to be an opportunity to sit down and talk properly. Nick had gone now, but Sophie didn't want to force the issue just before her father's party. Announcing that they weren't getting married after all would put a dampener on the evening, to say the least.

And tomorrow it would be too late. It would be fine, Sophie tried to convince herself. She and Bram *had* talked about things. They were friends, and they could be honest with each other. If Bram didn't want to marry her, he would say so.

Wouldn't he?

For want of anything else to wear, Sophie put on the flame-coloured dress again. It was bitterly cold. In spite of the sun, the snow hadn't melted at all, and the ground was icy beneath her feet as she walked towards the front door. At least there was no problem with mud tonight. No excuse for Bram to carry her again either.

This was her father's night, Sophie told herself fiercely when they arrived at Glebe Farm, and she wasn't going to think about anything else. So she smiled and laughed and made a fuss of him, and was pleased to see that he was enjoying himself, in his own taciturn way.

Her mother was in her element, of course. She loved having everybody there, and Sophie was touched at the effort she had made to make this a special day for Joe. Her parents were very different characters, but they understood each other and their marriage had endured. Would she and Bram still be married after thirty-three years?

Even if it didn't work out she would always be glad that she'd been here tonight for her father. It was all very Christmassy, with the scent of pine cones burning on the open fire and carols playing in the background. They even had mulled wine.

'Not too much for you two, though,' Harriet said, wagging her finger jovially at Bram and Sophie. 'It's very potent, and we don't want you with hangovers tomorrow!'

Sophie smiled and tried not to notice how close Melissa and Bram seemed to be. It wasn't anything they said, or anything they did. It was just a feeling she had when she saw them together. Nick was moody, and Melissa had been on edge when they arrived, but her sister relaxed perceptibly as Bram teased her and made a point of drawing her into the conversation.

She shouldn't be jealous because Bram was taking the trouble to make her sister feel better, Sophie told herself. Melissa had always brought out the protective instincts in Bram, and nothing was going to change that. It didn't necessarily mean that he was still in love with her.

Sitting beside her father, Sophie reminded herself of what Bram had said about moving on. He wanted to forget the past, he had said. Melissa's marriage to Nick, followed by his mother's death, had convinced him to put his love for Melissa behind him and start afresh, make a new life with Sophie.

Sophie wanted to believe him—but how could he stop loving Melissa when Melissa was right there, so beautiful and so needy? It was too much to expect Bram to remember his determination to move on with Sophie when Melissa was gazing at him with her lovely violet eyes and blossoming at his attention.

'You're very quiet, love.' Her father broke into Sophie's thoughts. 'Is everything all right?'

'Of course.' Sophie smiled brightly and squeezed his hand, hoping that her face hadn't betrayed her as she watched Bram and her sister.

Joe's gaze had followed hers, and his eyes rested thoughtfully on Melissa, who was laughing at something Bram had said.

'I sometimes think you didn't get all the attention you should have done when you were growing up,' he said to Sophie. 'Melissa was never as strong or as independent as you, and she seemed to need looking after in a way that you didn't. You always looked out for her too, even when you were just a little girl yourself. Maybe we all looked after Melissa too much,' said Joe. 'It might have been better to let her find her own way sometimes, instead of always relying on someone else.'

'She's got Nick to look after her now.'

'Ye-es.' Joe sounded a bit doubtful as he glanced at Nick, who was talking to Harriet and shooting jealous glances in Melissa's direction. It didn't take much to guess that he suspected the closeness that Sophie had seen between his wife and Bram, and he didn't care for it any more than she did.

'I'm just glad you're marrying Bram,' Joe said to Sophie. 'Now you'll have someone to look after you for a change.'

Sophie smiled, but her heart twisted. She didn't need Bram to look after her; she needed him to love her the way she loved him. But, seeing him with Melissa tonight, she was increasingly unsure that she was going to get what she wanted now more than anything else.

'I'm fine, Dad,' she said. 'But we shouldn't be talking about me anyway. Or Melissa. This is *your* night!'

'Yes, and it means a lot to me that you and Melissa are here,' Joe told her. 'All your mother and I ever wanted was for you both to be happy.'

'I know, Dad, and we are.'

'Are you, Sophie? Really?'

'Really,' she said firmly. 'I'm getting married tomorrow. I couldn't be happier.'

This evening was to celebrate her father's birthday, and she wasn't going to spoil it by so much as a suggestion of any doubts.

To convince him, Sophie exerted herself to be on sparkling form for the rest of the evening. Bram helped her to keep the conversation light and cheerful, but Nick contributed little, and Melissa was suspiciously brighteyed, with a feverish edge to her smile that worried Sophie.

'I'll clear away and make some coffee,' Melissa said, jumping up at the end of the meal as if she couldn't wait for a chance to get away. 'No, Mum, you've done enough—and, Nick, you'd better stay off that knee.'

'I'll give you a hand,' said Bram, and got to his feet before Sophie could offer.

Melissa smiled at him gratefully. 'What would we do without you, Bram?'

There was a momentary silence after they had gathered up the pudding dishes and disappeared in the direction of the kitchen. Nick looked sour, and as if he were about to make some comment, but Sophie forestalled him, turning quickly to her mother with a question about the catering arrangements for the next day.

As she had predicted, that kept Harriet occupied for some time, but eventually even her mother noticed how long Bram and Melissa were taking.

'What *are* they doing in there? I hope they're not doing all the washing up.'

'I hope the washing up is all they're doing,' muttered Nick under his breath.

Hoping that her parents hadn't heard, Sophie pushed back her chair abruptly. 'I'll go and see if they need a hand.'

The kitchen was empty when she walked in, but she could hear voices in the utility room. Without thinking, Sophie went over—only to stop dead in the doorway, her heart freezing at the sight of Bram holding Melissa in his arms, his brown head bent towards her golden one.

Bram had his back to the door, and neither of them was aware of Sophie watching, rigid with despair.

'It's not too late,' he was saying. 'Just tell him that you've changed your mind.'

'I'm not sure I can,' Melissa wept into his shoulder.

'You can if you really want to,' said Bram tenderly. 'It's never too late to say you've made a mistake.'

Sophie turned before she overheard any more, and walked back across the kitchen. 'Hey, what are you two doing in here?' she called from the door, as if she had just arrived from the dining room. She felt sick inside, but her voice sounded perfectly normal. She was not going to provoke a scene on her father's birthday, whatever happened. 'We're gasping for our coffee!'

Bram appeared out of the utility room, and if Sophie hadn't known better she would have sworn his expression was tinged with relief. 'Just coming,' he said cheerfully. 'We've got everything in the dishwasher.'

'Sorry we've been so long.' Melissa appeared beside him. She looked as if she had been crying, but—typically—it only made her look more beautiful and fragile than ever. When Sophie cried her skin went red and blotchy, her eyes puffed up and she looked awful, but not Melissa.

'You two take the coffee through,' she said. 'I won't be a minute.' She disappeared upstairs, presumably to repair any sign of tears.

Avoiding Bram's eyes, Sophie picked up the jug of coffee and carried it through to the dining room. She needed to talk to him and find out what was going on with Melissa—but when? More than anything she wanted to go back to Haw Gill with him that night, to be alone with him and to talk quietly, but her mother was adamant.

'You're staying here tonight, Sophie. There's too much to do tomorrow morning. And anyway, everyone knows it's unlucky to see your groom before you get to the church.'

So Sophie had to say goodbye to him in front of everybody. Bram hesitated for a moment, looking down into her eyes, then dropped a light, almost perfunctory kiss on her lips. 'Don't be late tomorrow,' was all he said.

It was strange being back in her old room, with her wedding dress hanging up behind the door. Sophie lay awake, looking at it, wishing that Bram was there so that she could hold onto him. When his arms were around her she felt safe. Alone, it was too easy to lose her nerve and feel desperately unsure that she was doing the right thing.

Again and again Sophie reminded herself about the deal they had made. They would build their marriage on friendship and would accept that neither could have what they really wanted. What was so wrong with that?

The trouble was that she had changed. Sophie realised now that what she really wanted was Bram. The balance had shifted and they weren't equal any more. It had made sense when they'd both thought they wanted someone they couldn't have. As long as Sophie had been in love with Nick she had understood what Bram felt for Melissa and believed that they were doing the right thing, throwing their lot in together.

But she wasn't in love with Nick any more. It was Bram she wanted now, and everything was different.

Sophie tossed and turned all night. She wanted to marry Bram, she wanted to be with him for ever, but she wanted him to love her too. How could she marry him if he still yearned for Melissa? Bram had said that he didn't, but what she had seen and heard tonight told a different story. It had sounded to Sophie as if Melissa might have changed her mind. As if Bram might, after all this time, have a chance to be with the woman he really loved.

She thought about how long she and Bram had been friends, about the times they had talked and laughed together, the times he had comforted her and teased her and been exactly what she needed him to be. She couldn't be truly happy if he wasn't. If Bram did have a chance to be with Melissa, should she—*could* she—stand in his way?

By morning, Sophie was looking drawn and haggard. She managed to get as far as putting her wedding dress on, but the sheen on the ivory material made her skin look dull and lifeless when she looked in the mirror, and her sister's radiantly beautiful reflection only made the contrast crueller.

Melissa seemed to have thrown off her nervousness of the night before, and was calm and loving as she helped her sister to get ready. Sophie was puzzled. Surely Melissa wouldn't be like this if she were helping Sophie to marry the man she herself loved?

Then Sophie thought about the effort *she* had made to make Melissa's wedding day special for her. She hadn't wanted her beloved sister to guess how much she was suffering so she had been bright and cheerful all day, and she didn't think anyone had guessed that her heart was breaking.

Except Bram. He had known, and he had been there for her.

'Do you think I'm doing the right thing?' she asked Melissa abruptly.

'Marrying Bram?' Melissa looked shocked. 'Of course I do. You're such good friends, and you know each other so well. How could it *not* be the right thing?'

'Is friendship enough, though?'

'I think it matters more than you know.' Melissa pulled up the zip on Sophie's dress and looked at her sister soberly in the mirror. 'You know, being married isn't as easy as you think it's going to be. You think that loving someone desperately will be enough, but I'm not sure that it is,' she confessed.

She hesitated, then smiled at Sophie. 'But you'll be all right. Bram's a wonderful man. He's kind and he's loving and he's constant—and those things are more important than anything.'

Melissa looked away before Sophie could see the tears standing in her eyes. 'I…I just hope you appreciate what you've got,' she said, her voice breaking slightly.

Sophie stared at her sister in the mirror. Could Melissa be regretting the choice she had made? It had sounded like that when she'd overheard her talking to Bram last night, but Sophie hadn't wanted to believe it. Was she really thinking of leaving Nick—of telling him, as Bram had urged her, that she didn't love him any more?

She couldn't ask Melissa outright if she wished that she could marry Bram instead. Melissa would deny it absolutely. It had been hard enough for her to accept that Sophie would give up Nick. She'd never accept that Sophie would give up Bram for her too.

But what about Bram? If he wanted Melissa, and could have Melissa, Sophie didn't want to be the reason it couldn't work. If she married him, he would never leave her. Sophie knew Bram. So did Melissa. *You always do what you say you're going to do,* she had told him when she'd picked Nick up from Haw Gill. If Bram said that he would be faithful to Sophie till death did them part, that was what he would be.

Even if it broke his heart to see Melissa alone once more, and to know how close he might have been to having his heart's desire.

'You look a little pale,' said Melissa, peering at her in concern. 'Why don't I get my make-up? We can do something about those shadows under your eyes, at least.'

Sophie studied her reflection as Melissa went off to

find her cosmetics bag. The wedding dress in the mirror seemed to mock her. This was a farce. What was she thinking of—marrying a man in love with her own sister? How could she ever possibly have thought that it would work? She couldn't do it to Bram, and she couldn't do it to herself.

She couldn't just sit there, Sophie realised. She couldn't sit there calmly and let Melissa conceal the shadows under her eyes. They were there for a reason. She couldn't pick up her bouquet, take her father's arm and walk down the aisle to meet Bram without talking to him.

And if she was going to talk to him before the wedding she would have to do it now.

Suddenly galvanized into action, Sophie ran downstairs in her stockinged feet. She could hear Melissa talking to her mother somewhere. There was no one around to stop her and ask her questions.

A beautiful bride's bouquet had been delivered that morning and was sitting on the kitchen table. Sophie ignored it, scrabbling desperately in the bowl where her parents kept their keys.

'What is it, love?' Joe had come into the kitchen, his tie hanging loose around his neck, and his weatherbeaten face creased in concern as he looked at her.

'Where are your car keys, Dad?'

'They're here,' he said, putting his hand on them straight away. 'Why?'

'I need to see Bram,' said Sophie tensely. 'I need to see him now. Can I take your car?'

After one look at her face, Joe didn't bother to argue. 'I'll take you,' he said. 'You're not driving on these roads in that state.'

'Oh, thank you, Dad,' she said fervently. 'Can we go now?'

He looked down at her feet. 'What about your shoes?'

She couldn't face going upstairs, encountering Melissa or her mother, answering their questions. 'I'll wear Mum's boots,' she said, dragging on a pair of her father's thick woollen socks and thrusting her feet into the rubber boots. They looked absurd under the wedding dress, but Sophie didn't care.

She ran out to where her father had the car started already. As she jumped in beside him she caught a glimpse of her mother at the window, gesticulating wildly.

'Can we hurry, Dad?'

'Not on these roads, lass.'

Joe said no more, and asked not a single question as he drove carefully up to Haw Gill on roads that were narrower and more treacherous than usual because of the snow. Sophie was glad of his silence. Her heart was thumping so hard she wouldn't have been able to hear anyway.

It was another beautiful day. The snow piled up by the roadside glittered in the pale winter sunshine, and the light over the frozen moors was dazzling. In a monochrome landscape the bare trees stood stark against the whiteness, their branches petrified in ice.

They saw Bram coming down from the moor in his tractor as they drove into the farmyard. The stock still had to be fed and checked, even if you were getting married—although Bram was cutting it fine if he were to be showered and changed and waiting at the church in an hour's time.

'Do you want me to wait?'

'No,' said Sophie. 'No, you'd better go and calm

Mum down. Tell her not to worry. It's just something I've got to do.' She opened her door, turning back on an impulse to kiss her father's cheek. 'Thanks, Dad.'

With a nod, Joe turned the car round and drove off as Bram brought the tractor to an abrupt halt. Jumping down, he stopped and stared at Sophie, standing ridiculously on the frozen mud of the yard in her wedding dress and Wellington boots. Bess, with no inhibitions, ran over to greet the woman who had let her sleep in front of the fire, tail wagging happily.

'Sophie!' Bram was wearing his old working trousers and a thick jumper with bits of hay sticking to it, and his voice was tense with apprehension. 'What are you doing here?'

'I had to see you.' Sophie bent to quieten Bess, shaking as much from nerves as from the biting cold.

He strode towards her. 'What's happened?'

'I...I have to be sure that you want to do this, Bram. That you want to marry me.'

Bram stopped a few feet from her, his brows drawn together. 'Why would I have changed my mind?'

'Melissa,' said Sophie simply.

'*Melissa?* What's she been saying to you?'

'Nothing. I saw you with her last night, when you were making the coffee.'

Bram opened his mouth to answer, then paused. 'What exactly did you see?'

'I saw you holding her.' Sophie hugged herself against the cold. 'I heard you telling her that it wasn't too late,' she rushed on. 'You said that it was never too late, Bram, but it will be too late if we get married today. I want you to know that it's not too late to change your mind. If you want to be with Melissa, if she's what you really want, it's better that we call the wedding off now.'

'Is that what *you* want to do?' said Bram slowly.

'No,' she said, incurably honest. 'But I want you to be happy.'

Closing the gap between then, Bram took her hands in a firm, warm clasp. 'Do you mean that, Sophie?'

She nodded, not meeting his eyes. 'I don't want to marry you if you're not going to be happy,' she muttered.

'Does my happiness really matter to you that much?'

Sophie swallowed, very conscious of his hands holding hers. 'Yes. I want you to be honest, Bram.'

'All right,' he said. 'To be absolutely honest, there's only one thing I need to make me happy.'

She made herself look up into his eyes, bracing herself to hear that he wanted Melissa to leave Nick.

'And that's you,' said Bram.

There was a frozen pause. Sophie stared at him, not sure that she had heard correctly. 'Me?'

'Yes, you,' he said. 'You're all I want and all I need. You asked me if I want to marry you today, and I do, but what I want even more than that is for you to love me, Sophie, the way I so desperately love you.'

'You love *me*?' Sophie repeated blankly, afraid to let herself believe even then.

Bram smiled at her expression. 'I'm afraid so,' he said. 'It's not part of our deal, I know. We agreed that we would be good friends. But, since you're asking me to be honest, Sophie, I have to tell you that being friends isn't enough for me.'

His grip on her hands tightened and he pulled her closer. 'I know you'll always be my friend, but I want more than that. I want you in my heart and in my life and in my bed as well. If you really want to make me happy, Sophie darling, all you have to do is to tell me that's where you want to be too.'

Sophie drew an unsteady breath as happiness tumbled dizzily through her. It was wonderful to be able to tell the truth at last. 'That's where I want to be, Bram,' she said shakily. 'That's what I want more than anything else in the world.'

He kissed her then, a hard, hungry kiss, and Sophie flung her arms round him and melted into him, delirious with the sheer joy of knowing that he was hers and he loved her.

'Oh, Bram,' she sighed, blizzarding kisses along his jaw, clinging to his wonderfully solid body, loving the taste of his mouth and the touch of his hands and the feel of his arms around her. 'I've been so unsure about everything. I thought you wanted to be with Melissa. When I overheard you last night it sounded as if you were persuading her that it wasn't too late for her to leave Nick for you.'

Bram tightened his hold on her. 'Absolutely not,' he said, horrified at the very thought. 'Melissa doesn't want to leave Nick; she loves him.'

'Then why has she seemed so tense and unhappy?'

'I don't think Nick realised what it would be like to be married. He was carried away by Melissa's beauty, but now that he's got her he feels tied down. Melissa says that whenever they go out he finds someone to flirt with.'

'Like he did with me at that engagement dinner?'

'Exactly,' said Bram. 'I think he's probably just beating his chest to prove that he's still male, but it hurts Melissa. I tried to encourage her to tell him that she wouldn't put up with it any more, but she was afraid that if she did Nick would leave. Last night I finally convinced her that she had to at least talk to him.'

Sophie leant her head against Bram's shoulder and kissed his throat. 'Is that what you were talking about for so long?'

'I could see that Melissa was wound up,' he tried to explain. 'She was feeling desperate about Nick, but she didn't want to say anything to spoil our engagement or your father's party. Nick was furious with her for calling the rescue services when he was lost, and she was at the end of her tether last night. It was obvious that she was on edge and needed someone to talk to.'

'Why didn't she talk to me?' said Sophie, a little hurt.

'She didn't feel that she could, after everything that happened with Nick. It would have been very awkward. We've always got on well, and I seemed to be the only one she *could* talk to.'

Sophie pulled back slightly to look at Bram. 'Are you still in love with her?' she made herself ask.

'I love Melissa,' he said, 'but I'm not *in* love with her any more. I don't think I have been for a very long time. I was used to the idea of loving her more than anything else.

'Then you came back, and I realised what it meant to really fall in love. It wasn't what I expected at all. This isn't what I felt for Melissa, Sophie,' he said earnestly. 'This is so much more real, and because it is I need you and want you and love you so much more. I told myself it would be fine being just friends, but it wasn't. I hated seeing you with Nick, wondering if you still loved him as much as you always said that you did. I wasn't sure— I couldn't believe you still could be—but you seemed determined to be friends with me and nothing else.'

'Only because you were,' Sophie protested, still strug-

gling to take in the wonderful, incredible, joyous fact
that he loved her—*her*. If it hadn't been for the cold
seeping up through her rubber boots she would have
been afraid that she was dreaming.

'I did love Nick,' she admitted. 'I loved him desperately for a while. But I don't love him any more, and I
never loved him the way I love you, Bram. I can see
now that what I felt for him was a kind of obsession.
But you…you're part of me. You always have been and
you always will be.'

She kissed him again, thrilled to know that she could,
and that he would kiss her back.

'I can't believe that loving you was right in front of
me all the time,' she said, kissing her way up his throat
and along his jaw. 'All those years and I didn't see it
until the other day, and now…now I can't see anything
else. There's just you. Only you. You're all that matters.'

She wrapped her arms around his back, rejoicing at
the feel of the powerful muscles flexing beneath her
touch, wondering if it was too cold to pull his shirt free
and let her hands drift over his skin. She wasn't feeling
cold at all now. Quite the opposite.

'Bram,' she murmured between kisses.

'Mmm?'

'Remember how you told me that if I wanted you to
make love to me all I had to do was say?'

He smiled against her ear. 'I do remember that, yes.'

'Can I drop it into the conversation now?'

Bram laughed and took her face between her hands.
'You don't think you might like to go and get married
first?' he suggested. 'I could make an honest woman of
you…and it would be a shame to waste all your mother's
planning.'

'The wedding!' Sophie jumped back in comical dismay. 'Mum's going to kill me!'

'We've still got twenty-five minutes,' said Bram, looking at his watch. 'We can do it. Ring her while I shower and get changed. Tell her we'll meet them at the church.'

Her parents were waiting for them at the church door as they drove up in the old Land Rover. Joe beamed at the sight of Sophie's radiant face, and watched indulgently as Bram gave her a lingering kiss. 'In you go,' he said, jerking his head towards the church with a grin. 'I'll bring her in in a minute!'

Harriet was rather tight-lipped, but too relieved that a last-minute cancellation had been averted to say too much as she fussed around Sophie. 'Here's the bouquet, and the flowers for your hair. Oh, dear, look at the state of it… Has anyone got a comb? And is that hay on your skirt, Sophie?'

She flicked it off disapprovingly while Sophie stood docile, thinking that her mother had borne enough that morning. 'Now, is that everything?' She stood back to inspect her daughter critically from top to toe, to reassure herself that she had done the best that she could.

Until she came to Sophie's feet.

'Sophie,' she said in an awful voice, 'tell me that you're not wearing Wellington boots under your wedding dress!'

'I just grabbed the first thing I could find,' said Sophie, peering down at the black rubber boots, liberally splattered with dried mud, that peeked out from beneath the ivory silk.

Harriet gave a small moan. 'We'll have to go back for your shoes. We must have forgotten them in all the rush.'

'No,' said Sophie. 'We're late already. I'll go as I am.'

'No daughter of mine is going up the aisle in gumboots!' said Harriet, scandalised at the very idea.

'I'll take them off, then.' Sophie was already stepping on the back of one boot to pull her foot free. Her father's old socks were thick enough to keep the chill off the soles of her feet. 'I'll get married in my socks,' she said, and took her father's arm with a brilliant smile.

'I'm ready,' she said, and he led her into the church.

Bram was waiting at the altar, and the look on his face as he saw her told Sophie everything she needed to know. Her heart swelling with happiness, she took her place beside him and smiled back at him. What more could she ask for at Christmas? Bram was everything that she needed. Her best friend. Her lover.

Her husband.

Introducing a brand-new miniseries

FOR *Love* OR MONEY

This is romance on the red carpet...

For Love or Money is the ultimate reading experience
for the reader who has a taste for tales of wealth and
celebrity and the accompanying gossip and scandal!

Look out for the special covers
and
these upcoming titles:

Coming in November:

SALE OR RETURN BRIDE
by Sarah Morgan

#2500

Coming in December:

TAKEN BY THE HIGHEST BIDDER
by Jane Porter

#2508

Harlequin Presents®
The ultimate emotional experience!

HARLEQUIN®
Presents

Seduction and Passion Guaranteed!

www.eHarlequin.com   HPSORB

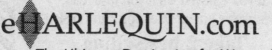

Coming Next Month

#3871 A MOST SUITABLE WIFE Jessica Steele

Taye Trafford's flatmate has run off leaving Taye to pay all the bills alone! Her solution: renting a room to Magnus Ashthorpe. But Magnus hasn't moved in because he wants somewhere to live—he believes Taye is the mistress who has caused his sister's heartbreak! Magnus soon discovers Taye's kind and innocent personality—in fact, perhaps she'd make a most suitable wife…?

#3872 A NANNY FOR KEEPS Liz Fielding

Jacqui Moore is on the run—from being a nanny! But when she meets little orphaned Maisie she's railroaded into being her nanny for just one night. Nights turn into weeks…and all too soon, the master of the house, magnificent yet scarred Harry Talbot, and little Maisie, have stolen her heart…and there's nowhere left to run!

Heart to Heart

#3873 CHRISTMAS GIFT: A FAMILY Barbara Hannay

Wealthy bachelor Hugh Strickland is stunned to discover he has a daughter. He wants to bring Ivy home—but he's terrified! Hugh hardly knows Jo Berry, but he pleads with her to help him—surely the ideal solution would be to give each other the perfect Christmas gift: a family.…

#3874 TAKING ON THE BOSS Darcy Maguire

Tahlia has tried so hard to prove herself at work—but suddenly gorgeous Case Darrington has stolen her promotion from right under her feet! Tahlia is determined to prove that it should be *her* sitting in Case's chair—but that means getting up-close-and-personal with her new boss!

Office Gossip